Jennifer's Journey From Tragedy to Triumph

Daniel Mendez

Published by Daniel Mendez, 2024.

This is a work of fiction. Similarities to real people, places, or events are entirely coincidental.

JENNIFER'S JOURNEY FROM TRAGEDY TO TRIUMPH

First edition. January 30, 2024.

ISBN: 979-8224415434

Written by Daniel Mendez.

1. A Happy Family: Introducing Jennifer and her mother, Emily, in their loving home.

2. Unveiling Secrets: Jennifer accidentally discovers her mother's sexual orientation.

3. Acceptance and Love: Jennifer embraces her mother's truth and supports her.

4. Tragic Night: Jennifer witnesses her mother being stabbed to death in front of her.

5. Mourning and Grief: Jennifer struggles to cope with the loss and trauma.

6. Moving In with Relatives: Jennifer goes to live with her aunt and uncle.

7. New Beginnings: Starting a new school year without her mother.

8. Finding a Support System: Jennifer befriends a counselor who helps her heal.

9. Unearthing Clues: Jennifer starts investigating her mother's murder.

10. Facing the Truth: Jennifer uncovers shocking details about the crime.

11. A Mother's Legacy: Remembering Emily's dreams and aspirations.

12. Path to Revenge: Jennifer contemplates seeking justice for her mother.

13. Legal Battles: Jennifer learns about the challenges of pursuing the case.

14. The Power of Forgiveness: Jennifer wrestles with her feelings towards the perpetrator.

15. Discovering Finance: Jennifer's interest in business and finance grows.

16. Mentorship: Jennifer finds guidance from a successful businesswoman.

17. Educational Pursuits: Jennifer excels in her studies and gains scholarships.

18. University Life: Jennifer starts her business and finance degree.

19. First Taste of Entrepreneurship: Jennifer launches a small online venture.

20. Overcoming Challenges: Jennifer faces setbacks and learns valuable lessons.

21. Networking and Connections: Jennifer expands her professional circle.

22. Rising Ambitions: Jennifer dreams of starting her own business.

23. Startup Ventures: Jennifer's first attempts at launching a business.

24. Learning from Failure: Jennifer experiences a business setback.

25. Rebuilding Confidence: Jennifer perseveres and learns from her mistakes.

26. Innovative Idea: Jennifer conceives a groundbreaking business concept.

27. Seeking Investors: Jennifer pitches her idea to potential backers.

28. The Journey Begins: Jennifer secures funding and launches her business.

29. Navigating Entrepreneurship: Jennifer faces the realities of running a company.

30. Balancing Act: Jennifer juggles work, studies, and personal life.

31. Love and Relationships: Jennifer explores romantic interests.

32. Empowering Others: Jennifer mentors aspiring entrepreneurs.

33. Expanding Horizons: Jennifer's business gains traction and recognition.

34. International Opportunities: Jennifer explores global markets.

35. Scaling Up: Jennifer's company experiences rapid growth.

36. Dealing with Competition: Jennifer faces challenges from rival businesses.

37. Ethical Dilemmas: Jennifer makes tough decisions in her business.

38. Making a Difference: Jennifer incorporates social responsibility into her company.

39. Personal Growth: Jennifer reflects on her journey and growth.

40. Family Reunion: Jennifer reconnects with estranged relatives.

41. Legacy of Strength: Jennifer honors her mother's memory.

42. Facing the Past: Jennifer confronts her mother's murderer.

43. Healing Wounds: Jennifer finds closure and forgiveness.

44. Media Spotlight: Jennifer's success story attracts media attention.

45. Sharing Her Story: Jennifer becomes an advocate for resilience.

46. Philanthropic Ventures: Jennifer gives back to her community.

47. Exploring New Avenues: Jennifer diversifies her business interests.

48. Overcoming Burnout: Jennifer learns to balance her demanding life.

49. Unexpected Alliances: Jennifer collaborates with surprising partners.

50. Business Innovations: Jennifer continues to disrupt her industry.

51. New Challenges: Jennifer navigates economic downturns.

52. Adapting and Thriving: Jennifer's business weathers storms.

53. A Personal Triumph: Jennifer achieves a significant milestone.

54. Reconnecting with Love: Jennifer's romantic relationship evolves.

55. Looking Ahead: Jennifer contemplates her future endeavors.

56. Inspiring the Next Generation: Jennifer mentors young entrepreneurs.

Chapter 1: A Happy Family

In a cozy suburban house nestled amidst a row of blossoming cherry trees, Jennifer and her mother, Emily, shared a bond that radiated warmth and joy. The house, adorned with ivy climbing its walls and a white picket fence, exuded an inviting charm that mirrored the love within its walls.

The mornings often began with the aroma of freshly brewed coffee wafting through the air, as Emily, a skilled baker, prepared her signature cinnamon buns that Jennifer adored. The sound of laughter echoed through the kitchen as Jennifer, a teenager with a vibrant spirit, helped her mother with the baking, their flour-covered hands playfully patting each other's cheeks.

Their conversations spanned from the trivialities of school life to profound discussions about dreams and aspirations. Emily was more than a mother; she was a confidante and a friend. The living room was adorned with framed photographs that captured their most cherished moments: Jennifer's first day of school, the impromptu picnics at the park, and the radiant smiles that mirrored the bond they shared.

Evenings were a time of togetherness. They would curl up on the couch with a well-loved novel or watch classic movies, a shared bowl of popcorn nestled between them. As the sun dipped below the horizon, casting hues of orange and pink across the sky, Jennifer would often snuggle into her mother's side, feeling safe and cherished.

Emily, a strong advocate for open communication, had fostered an environment where Jennifer felt comfortable expressing her thoughts and emotions. No topic was off-limits, and this openness allowed Jennifer to grow into a confident and compassionate young woman.

One wall in Jennifer's bedroom was adorned with an array of art projects – colorful canvases that bore witness to their shared creative endeavors. From finger-painting as a child to experimenting with watercolors as a teenager, their joint artistic ventures had resulted in a kaleidoscope of memories that adorned Jennifer's personal space.

As bedtime approached, Jennifer would often kneel by her bedside, her small hands folded together as she whispered a heartfelt prayer. Emily would join her, the soft cadence of their voices mingling with the quiet evening breeze that rustled the leaves outside.

The harmony that enveloped their home was a testament to Emily's unwavering love and Jennifer's boundless affection. Theirs was a partnership that stood the test of time, a sanctuary where they found solace and support in each other's presence.

But little did they know, their idyllic world was about to face an unexpected turn. As Jennifer's life was intricately woven with the threads of her mother's love, the tapestry they had created would soon be challenged by a series of events that would push Jennifer to her limits, ultimately leading her on a journey of resilience and triumph.

Chapter 2: Unveiling Secrets

The soft glow of twilight bathed Jennifer's room as she sat at her desk, engrossed in a history assignment. It was during one of these quiet evenings that fate, in its enigmatic way, would introduce Jennifer to a secret that had long been kept hidden.

Lost in thought, Jennifer picked up an old photo album that lay beside her textbooks. The album's pages were filled with snapshots of birthdays, holidays, and family outings. She smiled as she flipped through the pages, reminiscing about the memories they held.

As Jennifer turned a page, a small, folded piece of paper slipped out from between the pages and fluttered to the floor. Curiosity piqued, she picked it up and unfolded it, her eyes scanning the neat handwriting.

"Dearest Emily," the letter began, revealing a heartfelt confession of love. Jennifer's heart quickened as she read on, realizing that the letter was not written by her father, who had passed away when she was just a child. Instead, it was a love letter from a woman named Lily.

Jennifer's mind swirled with a whirlwind of emotions – confusion, surprise, and a gnawing curiosity. She remembered Lily, a close friend of her mother's, who had visited their home often over the years. The pieces of the puzzle began to fall into place, and Jennifer realized the truth that had been carefully hidden: her mother, Emily, was gay.

The revelation held an odd mix of feelings for Jennifer. She felt a strange blend of admiration for her mother's courage in keeping her truth concealed, and yet a sense of unease at the idea that there were aspects of her mother's life she had never known. She wondered how Emily had navigated her emotions, kept this hidden, and carried on as a loving mother.

The following days were marked by a flurry of emotions for Jennifer. She observed her mother closely, trying to understand the layers that made up Emily's identity. She felt a growing need to talk to someone about what she had discovered but was torn between respecting her mother's privacy and seeking answers to her own questions.

Finally, one evening, as the sun began to set and cast long shadows through the living room, Jennifer mustered the courage to approach her mother. Emily was sitting on the porch, gazing out at the fading horizon, lost in her thoughts.

"Mom," Jennifer began tentatively, her voice catching in her throat.

Emily turned to her daughter, her eyes warm and understanding. "Yes, sweetheart?"

Jennifer took a deep breath. "I found a letter, Mom. A letter from Lily."

Emily's gaze softened, and she patted the empty seat beside her. Jennifer hesitated for a moment before sitting down. "I didn't mean to invade your privacy, Mom. I just... I want to understand."

Emily smiled gently. "I've always believed in being honest with you, Jennifer. Lily was someone very special to me. She was my partner, my confidante, and my closest friend."

As Emily began to share her story, Jennifer felt a flood of emotions – empathy, admiration, and a newfound appreciation for her mother's journey. The conversation opened doors to understanding, bridging the gap between Jennifer's curiosity and her mother's experiences.

In the wake of their conversation, Jennifer realized that their bond remained unshaken. If anything, it had grown stronger. Emily's vulnerability had given Jennifer a glimpse into the depths of her mother's heart, and in that moment, Jennifer knew that no matter the challenges they faced, their love would always endure.

And so, on that quiet evening, beneath the canvas of a sky painted with hues of orange and pink, Jennifer and Emily shared a moment of connection that would forever shape the path of Jennifer's journey from tragedy to triumph.

Chapter 3: Acceptance and Love

In the days that followed the discovery of her mother's secret, Jennifer's mind swirled with a myriad of thoughts and emotions. As the initial shock began to subside, a deep sense of compassion and empathy washed over her.

The memory of her mother's loving embrace and unwavering support throughout her own life echoed in Jennifer's heart. She knew that it was her turn now to be there for Emily. With a newfound determination, Jennifer set out to learn more about her mother's journey, seeking to understand the challenges she had faced and the strength it took to keep her truth hidden.

Late one evening, as they sat in the cozy living room, Jennifer took a deep breath and spoke softly, "Mom, can we talk?"

Emily looked up from her book, her eyes meeting Jennifer's with a warm smile. "Of course, sweetheart. What's on your mind?"

Jennifer hesitated for a moment, the weight of her words hanging in the air. "I've been thinking a lot about what you've been through, Mom. I want you to know that I support you, no matter what."

Tears glistened in Emily's eyes as she reached out to hold Jennifer's hand. "Thank you, Jennifer. Your understanding means the world to me."

As Emily began to share her story, Jennifer listened intently. She learned about the struggles Emily had faced – the fear of judgment, the uncertainty, and the journey towards self-acceptance. Jennifer's heart swelled with pride for her mother's resilience, and her admiration for Emily deepened.

Over the coming weeks, Jennifer actively sought out resources and information about LGBTQ+ issues. She immersed herself in books, articles, and documentaries, eager to broaden her understanding and provide her mother with the unwavering support she deserved.

One evening, Jennifer surprised Emily with a homemade dinner. The dining table was adorned with a colorful LGBTQ+ flag, and a candle flickered in the center, casting a warm glow. Emily's eyes welled up with emotion as she took in the sight.

"Jennifer, this is beautiful," Emily said, her voice choked with gratitude.

"I want you to know that I'm here for you, Mom," Jennifer said, her voice steady and reassuring. "I want to be a source of support, just like you've always been for me."

Emily reached across the table to clasp Jennifer's hand. "You already are, sweetheart. Your love and acceptance mean more to me than I can express."

Their dinner that evening was filled with heartfelt conversations and shared laughter. They talked about the importance of open-mindedness, compassion, and the significance of embracing one's true self.

As time went on, Jennifer and Emily's relationship flourished in new ways. They attended LGBTQ+ events together, participated in community initiatives, and engaged in conversations that deepened their connection. Jennifer found herself becoming an advocate for equality and acceptance, inspired by her mother's journey.

One day, as they walked hand in hand at a local Pride parade, Jennifer turned to Emily with a smile. "You know, Mom, you've always been my role model. But now, you're an inspiration to so many others too."

Tears glistened in Emily's eyes as she hugged Jennifer tightly. "And you, my dear, are the embodiment of love and acceptance. You've embraced me with an open heart, and I couldn't be prouder of the person you've become."

In that moment, surrounded by the vibrant colors and celebratory spirit of the parade, Jennifer felt an overwhelming sense of fulfillment. She had not only embraced her mother's truth but had also become a beacon of acceptance and love herself. As their journey continued, Jennifer knew that their unbreakable bond would carry them through any challenges that lay ahead, united by the strength of their shared journey.

Chapter 4: Tragic Night

The moon hung low in the velvety sky, casting a silvery glow over the quiet suburban street. Jennifer's home, usually a haven of warmth and laughter, stood bathed in an eerie calmness that seemed to foreshadow the events about to unfold.

It was a night like any other, as Emily and Jennifer prepared for a quiet evening together. Emily had cooked a comforting meal, and the aroma of her culinary creations wafted through the air, promising an evening of shared stories and cherished moments.

As they sat down to dinner, the gentle hum of conversation filled the room. Emily's laughter danced like music, mingling with Jennifer's animated anecdotes from her day. The bond between mother and daughter was palpable, a tapestry of shared experiences and unbreakable love.

The clock ticked away, and the evening wore on. Jennifer could sense a faint unease in the air – a subtle shift that seemed to whisper of a looming darkness. Her instincts were heightened, and her heart raced for reasons she couldn't quite comprehend.

A sudden knock at the door shattered the tranquility of the night. Emily's expression tightened, a shadow of concern flitting across her face. "Stay here, Jennifer," she murmured, rising from her chair and moving towards the front door.

As Jennifer sat frozen at the dining table, a wave of anxiety washed over her. Her heart pounded in her chest, and a chilling sense of foreboding settled in the pit of her stomach. She strained to hear the muffled voices from the hallway, a guttural exchange that sent shivers down her spine.

Before she could process what was happening, the door swung open with a violent force. Jennifer's eyes widened in horror as a figure stepped into the room, a malicious glint in their eyes. A knife gleamed ominously in the dim light.

"Emily, no!" Jennifer's voice cracked as she screamed, a primal surge of adrenaline propelling her forward.

Time seemed to slow as Jennifer lunged towards her mother, her movements a blur of desperation and fear. The room erupted in chaos, a cacophony of anguished cries and shattering glass. Jennifer's hands reached out instinctively, her fingers grazing the hilt of the knife as she fought to wrest it away.

But the struggle was brief, and the world seemed to collapse in on itself. A guttural scream tore through the air, echoing Jennifer's heartbreak and terror. In the flickering light, she saw the unthinkable unfold before her eyes – her mother, Emily, collapsing to the ground, the cruel reality of violence staining the sanctuary they had called home.

Time stood still as Jennifer's world shattered into a million pieces. The air felt thick with grief, the weight of the tragedy pressing down on her chest until each breath felt like a struggle. The room spun, colors blurring into a nightmarish haze as Jennifer's mind grappled with the unfathomable.

Kneeling beside her mother's lifeless form, Jennifer's hands trembled as she reached out to touch Emily's still-warm cheek. Tears streamed down her face as she whispered her mother's name, a desperate plea for the impossible.

In the aftermath of the unfathomable horror, Jennifer clung to her mother's memory, the essence of their love serving as a fragile lifeline in a world suddenly devoid of light. The tragic night etched itself into Jennifer's soul, an indelible mark that would forever shape the course of her journey from the depths of despair to the relentless pursuit of triumph.

Chapter 5: Mourning and Grief

The days that followed the tragic night were a blur of heartache and disbelief. Jennifer moved through a world that felt surreal, as if the very fabric of reality had been torn apart. The once-familiar rooms of her home now seemed haunted by the memories of that fateful evening.

Grief settled over Jennifer like a heavy shroud, her every breath a reminder of the profound loss she had endured. The weight of her mother's absence was suffocating, a relentless ache that seemed to echo through every corner of her being.

Each day, Jennifer woke to a reality that felt like a cruel nightmare from which she couldn't escape. The simple routines that had once brought her comfort now served as painful reminders of a life forever changed. The scent of her mother's favorite perfume lingered in the air, an intangible presence that tugged at Jennifer's heart.

The outside world carried on, oblivious to Jennifer's anguish. Friends and neighbors offered condolences, their words a symphony of sympathy that felt distant and hollow. Jennifer appreciated their gestures, but the chasm of grief that consumed her was too vast to bridge with mere words.

Nights were the most difficult. As darkness descended, Jennifer found herself grappling with vivid nightmares that replayed the events of that tragic night. She would wake in a cold sweat, her heart racing and her mother's name on her lips, only to be met by the chilling silence of an empty house.

Jennifer's appetite waned, and the weight of grief began to take a visible toll on her. She withdrew from the world around her, retreating into the solitude of her room. The once-vibrant art projects that adorned her walls now seemed distant and untouched, a testament to the life that had been abruptly extinguished.

In the midst of her grief, Jennifer found solace in the small fragments of her mother's presence that remained. A handwritten recipe tucked away in a kitchen drawer, a worn book with a heartfelt inscription, and the soft echo of Emily's laughter in the wind – these were the lifelines that Jennifer clung to, the threads that connected her to the love that had shaped her world.

As Jennifer grappled with her loss, she also faced the aftermath of the trauma she had witnessed. Flashbacks of that horrifying night would seize her unexpectedly, plunging her into a vortex of fear and helplessness. The weight of survivor's guilt bore down on her, a relentless questioning of why she had been spared when her mother had been taken.

Seeking refuge from the torment of her thoughts, Jennifer began attending therapy sessions. With the guidance of a compassionate counselor, she started to navigate the turbulent waters of grief and trauma. Each session was a step toward understanding her emotions, a space where she could untangle the complex web of feelings that threatened to overwhelm her.

As Jennifer gradually opened up about her pain, she found herself surrounded by a support network that extended beyond her therapist. Friends and family rallied around her, offering a lifeline of compassion and understanding. While the pain of loss remained, the empathy of those who cared for her helped to ease the burden, if only slightly.

Through the haze of mourning, Jennifer began to explore ways to honor her mother's memory. She sifted through old photographs, created a scrapbook of cherished moments, and penned heartfelt letters to Emily that she placed in a memory box. These gestures were small but meaningful, a way to keep her mother's spirit alive in the midst of overwhelming sorrow.

As the days turned into weeks, Jennifer's journey through grief continued. It was a path fraught with pain and darkness, but she was determined to navigate it with the same resilience that her mother had instilled in her. Emily's love and guidance were a beacon of strength, a reminder that even in the depths of despair, there was a glimmer of hope that someday, somehow, Jennifer would find her way back to the light.

Chapter 6: Moving In with Relatives

The decision had been made amidst a backdrop of heartache and upheaval – Jennifer would leave behind the home that held a lifetime of memories and move in with her aunt and uncle. The once-familiar hallways and rooms had become a haunting labyrinth of grief, and the change was a necessary step in her journey toward healing.

As Jennifer's belongings were packed into boxes, the air seemed heavy with a sense of finality. Each item held a memory, a connection to the life she had known before tragedy struck. Her heart ached as she surveyed her room, the place where laughter had once danced in the air and dreams had taken shape.

The day of departure arrived, and the house that had been a sanctuary now stood silent, a witness to the countless emotions that had unfolded within its walls. Jennifer's aunt and uncle, faces etched with empathy, stood by her side as they said their goodbyes. The weight of the moment hung in the air, a bittersweet blend of sorrow and hope.

As Jennifer stepped out of her childhood home for what felt like the last time, her heart clenched with a mixture of grief and uncertainty. The journey to her new temporary residence was a silent one, the passing scenery a blur as Jennifer's thoughts swirled with a whirlwind of emotions.

Arriving at her aunt and uncle's home, Jennifer was greeted by open arms and warm embraces. The familiar scent of home cooked meals and the sounds of laughter filled the air, offering a stark contrast to the emptiness she had left behind. The guest room, adorned with welcoming touches, became Jennifer's new haven – a place to seek refuge and begin anew.

In the days that followed, Jennifer settled into her new routine. The bustling household provided a sense of normalcy that had been missing from her life, and the presence of her cousins added a touch of companionship that eased the solitude of her grief.

Mornings began with the aroma of fresh coffee and the sizzle of bacon in the kitchen. Evenings were marked by shared meals and animated conversations that filled the dining table with warmth and laughter. As Jennifer navigated her way through grief, her aunt and uncle provided a steady anchor of support, offering a listening ear and words of wisdom that helped to ease her pain.

Jennifer's days were a blend of introspection and interaction. She spent hours poring over photo albums and journals, reliving the cherished memories she had shared with her mother. It was a bittersweet ritual – a way to keep her mother's spirit alive while also acknowledging the profound void her absence had created.

Outside the walls of her temporary home, Jennifer's therapist became a crucial lifeline. Through their sessions, she learned to confront the trauma she had witnessed and the complex emotions that had taken root within her. Slowly but surely, Jennifer began to navigate the labyrinth of grief, armed with the tools she needed to move forward.

As the weeks turned into months, Jennifer's journey began to take on a new shape. She discovered strength she didn't know she possessed and a resilience that had been forged in the crucible of loss. Her bond with her aunt and uncle deepened, their unwavering support a testament to the power of family.

While the pain of her mother's absence remained a constant ache, Jennifer found solace in the love that surrounded her. The halls of her aunt and uncle's home, once unfamiliar, had become a place of refuge and renewal. With each passing day, Jennifer took one step closer to embracing her new reality, her mother's love a guiding light that illuminated the path ahead.

Chapter 7: New Beginnings

The summer sun cast a golden hue over the tree-lined streets as Jennifer prepared to embark on a new school year. The air was tinged with a crispness that signaled the approach of autumn, and as Jennifer donned her school uniform, a sense of both excitement and trepidation filled her heart.

The school, with its bustling hallways and familiar faces, was a stark reminder of the passage of time. It had been several months since Jennifer's world had been shattered, and yet the cycle of life continued – a reminder that even amidst grief, the world moved forward.

As Jennifer stepped through the school gates, she felt a mixture of emotions. The once-familiar routine of the first day of school felt both comforting and alien. The absence of her mother's reassuring presence was acutely felt, a void that seemed to echo through the corridors.

Entering her classroom, Jennifer was met with curious glances from her classmates. The word had spread – the girl who had faced an unimaginable tragedy was returning to school. Whispers and sympathetic glances followed her, a reminder that her journey was visible to those around her.

The bell rang, signaling the start of the school day. Jennifer took her seat, her gaze fixed on the empty desk beside her. It was a stark reminder of the companionship she had lost, the shared moments and inside jokes that had once made the classroom feel like a second home.

Throughout the day, Jennifer navigated the halls with a mixture of determination and vulnerability. Her interactions with classmates were a delicate dance – a balance between gratitude for their empathy and a desire for a semblance of normalcy. The hallway conversations, though brief, provided a connection to a world that had remained unchanged despite her personal turmoil.

Lunchtime brought a new challenge. The bustling cafeteria, once a place of camaraderie, now felt isolating. Jennifer navigated the sea of tables, her heart heavy as she searched for a place to sit. It was in that moment of uncertainty that a friendly voice cut through the noise.

"Jennifer, over here!" called a classmate from a nearby table. The warm smile and open invitation were a lifeline, and Jennifer gratefully joined her new companions. As they chatted and shared stories, Jennifer felt a glimmer of camaraderie – a reminder that new beginnings held the potential for connection and friendship.

Days turned into weeks, and Jennifer gradually settled into her new routine. The rhythm of school life provided a semblance of structure amidst the chaos of her emotions. Homework assignments, group projects, and extracurricular activities kept her occupied, serving as a temporary reprieve from the weight of her grief.

Outside of school, Jennifer continued to work through her feelings with her therapist. The weekly sessions provided a safe space for her to explore her emotions, from the sorrow that still consumed her to the moments of resilience that had begun to emerge. Through introspection and guidance, Jennifer learned to navigate the complexities of her grief and find the strength to move forward.

As autumn gave way to winter, Jennifer's journey took on a new significance. The changing seasons mirrored her own transformation – a gradual shift from darkness to the promise of renewal. With each passing day, she embraced the challenges that came her way, drawing strength from her mother's enduring love and the newfound connections she had forged.

The first school year without her mother was a testament to Jennifer's resilience. It was a chapter of new beginnings, marked by the courage to face adversity and the determination to honor her mother's memory. As the days grew longer and the world awakened from its winter slumber, Jennifer looked ahead to the promise of spring – a season of growth, renewal, and the unwavering pursuit of triumph.

Chapter 8: Finding a Support System

Amidst the turbulent sea of emotions that engulfed Jennifer's life, a beacon of light emerged in the form of a compassionate counselor named Dr. Campbell. Their paths crossed on a seemingly ordinary day, but the connection they forged would prove to be a lifeline in Jennifer's journey toward healing.

It was a crisp afternoon when Jennifer stepped into the cozy waiting room of Dr. Campbell's office. The walls adorned with soothing artwork and soft lighting created an atmosphere of comfort and tranquility. The scent of lavender lingered in the air, inviting a sense of calm that Jennifer hadn't felt in months.

As Jennifer sat down in the plush chair, she felt a mixture of apprehension and hope. The weight of her grief seemed to intensify in this safe space, where she knew she would confront the pain she had carried for so long. Moments later, the door opened, and Dr. Campbell walked in with a warm smile.

"Hello, Jennifer. I'm Dr. Campbell. It's a pleasure to meet you," she said, extending her hand.

Jennifer shook Dr. Campbell's hand, her nerves momentarily eased by the counselor's reassuring presence. "Thank you for seeing me," Jennifer replied, her voice soft.

Their conversations unfolded like a delicate dance, with Dr. Campbell guiding Jennifer through the labyrinth of her emotions. With each session, Jennifer shared her thoughts, fears, and memories – the fragments of her shattered world. Dr. Campbell listened with unwavering empathy, providing a space where Jennifer's pain could be acknowledged and validated.

Through their conversations, Jennifer began to peel back the layers of her grief. Dr. Campbell's gentle guidance encouraged Jennifer to explore the complex emotions that had taken root within her. It was a process that required vulnerability, but Jennifer found herself drawn to the therapeutic release that came with sharing her innermost thoughts.

Outside of the counseling sessions, Dr. Campbell introduced Jennifer to various coping strategies – mindfulness techniques, journaling, and deep breathing exercises. These tools became a lifeline, helping Jennifer navigate the moments of overwhelming emotion that often threatened to consume her.

One day, as Jennifer grappled with a particularly painful memory during a session, Dr. Campbell gently suggested a technique called grounding. Closing her eyes, Jennifer followed Dr. Campbell's guidance, focusing on the sensation of her feet against the floor and the rhythm of her breathing. In that moment, she felt a sense of control – a small victory over the waves of grief that had threatened to engulf her.

Beyond the therapeutic techniques, Jennifer found in Dr. Campbell a source of unwavering support and guidance. Their relationship evolved from a professional connection to a genuine bond of trust. Dr. Campbell became a confidante, a guiding light who helped Jennifer navigate the complexities of her grief with compassion and wisdom.

As the months passed, Jennifer's healing journey gained momentum. The weight of her grief began to lift, replaced by a growing sense of resilience and hope. Dr. Campbell's guidance empowered Jennifer to confront her trauma, process her emotions, and envision a future that held the promise of triumph.

Outside of the counseling office, Jennifer's newfound strength began to manifest in her daily life. She rekindled her love for art, using painting as a means of expression and healing. She also started participating in support groups for individuals who had experienced loss and trauma, finding solace in the shared experiences of others.

With Dr. Campbell's unwavering support and the tools she had acquired, Jennifer's journey toward healing was marked by profound transformation. The darkness that had once enveloped her began to recede, making way for a newfound sense of purpose and resilience. Jennifer's story became one of courage, determination, and the power of finding a support system that could guide her from the depths of despair to the boundless heights of triumph.

Chapter 9: Unearthing Clues

In the wake of her mother's tragic murder, Jennifer found herself consumed by a relentless need for answers. The unexplained violence that had shattered her world remained a haunting mystery, and the ache to uncover the truth grew stronger with each passing day.

Armed with determination and a sense of purpose, Jennifer embarked on a journey to unearth the clues that might lead her to the elusive answers she sought. The process was a delicate dance – a balance between the pain of revisiting the past and the hope of finding justice for her mother's memory.

Her first step was to immerse herself in the details surrounding the night of the tragedy. Jennifer revisited the scene of the crime, the place where her mother's life had been abruptly taken. She retraced her own steps, piecing together the fragments of memory that had been etched into her mind. It was a painful process, one that dredged up raw emotions, but Jennifer was determined to leave no stone unturned.

As Jennifer delved deeper, she began to connect the dots between the events leading up to her mother's murder. She reached out to friends, neighbors, and anyone who might have had insights into her mother's life. Conversations became a tapestry of memories and anecdotes, each thread contributing to a clearer picture of the woman her mother had been.

One name that surfaced repeatedly was that of Lily – her mother's close friend. Jennifer's curiosity was piqued. She remembered the love letter she had found, the one that had revealed her mother's hidden truth. Could Lily hold the key to understanding more about her mother's life and, potentially, the motive behind the tragedy?

With cautious optimism, Jennifer reached out to Lily, initiating a meeting that would be pivotal in her quest for answers. The encounter was marked by a mixture of anxiety and anticipation, the weight of unspoken questions hanging in the air. As they sat across from each other, Jennifer's heart raced.

"Lily, I need to understand," Jennifer began, her voice steady but filled with emotion. "I want to know everything – about you, about my mother, about that night."

Lily's eyes held a depth of emotion as she began to share her story. She spoke of a deep and profound love that had flourished between her and Jennifer's mother, Emily. She recounted the challenges they had faced, the joy they had shared, and the journey of self-discovery that had ultimately brought them together.

As Lily spoke, Jennifer felt a renewed connection to her mother's truth. The revelations were both heart-wrenching and affirming, a testament to the courage and resilience that had defined her mother's journey. And then, the conversation turned to the night of the murder.

Lily's voice trembled as she recounted her memories of that tragic evening. She spoke of an encounter with an unfamiliar figure, a heated exchange that had left her rattled and afraid. The pieces began to align, and Jennifer's mind raced with a surge of determination. Could this encounter be the missing puzzle piece – the clue that would lead her to the truth behind her mother's murder?

With Lily's guidance, Jennifer delved deeper into the mystery. She reached out to law enforcement, collaborating with detectives who had worked on the case. Together, they revisited the evidence, reexamining the details that had once been scrutinized. Jennifer's persistence and determination breathed new life into the investigation, reinvigorating the search for justice.

Days turned into weeks, and Jennifer's efforts yielded a breakthrough. A previously overlooked piece of evidence – a security camera footage from a nearby establishment – provided a glimpse of the figure who had confronted Lily on that fateful night. The image was grainy, but it held the promise of a lead – a potential clue that could finally shed light on the identity of her mother's murderer.

As Jennifer stood before the detective, the photograph in her hand, a mixture of hope and fear coursed through her veins. The path ahead was uncertain, fraught with challenges and uncertainties. Yet, for the first time since her mother's murder, Jennifer felt a glimmer of possibility – a belief that the truth was within reach, waiting to be unearthed.

With unwavering resolve, Jennifer's journey of investigation and discovery had begun. The road ahead would be marked by twists and turns, but her determination to honor her mother's memory and seek justice would fuel her every step. As she delved deeper into the labyrinth of clues, Jennifer knew that she was not alone – her mother's love and the support of those who believed in her quest would guide her through the shadows toward the relentless pursuit of truth.

Chapter 10: Facing the Truth

The air was charged with tension as Jennifer sat in the dimly lit interrogation room, the photograph of the mysterious figure resting before her. The detective, a seasoned investigator named Detective Reynolds, watched her closely, his expression a mixture of seriousness and empathy.

"Jennifer," Detective Reynolds began, his voice measured, "this is a crucial moment in our investigation. The image you provided could be the key to unlocking the truth. But I need to prepare you – the details we uncover might be difficult to hear."

Jennifer nodded, her heart pounding in her chest. She knew that she was on the precipice of discovering the truth behind her mother's murder, and despite the fear that gnawed at her, she was determined to face whatever revelations lay ahead.

As Detective Reynolds began to explain, Jennifer learned that the figure captured in the photograph had been identified as a man named Robert Davis – a name that sent a shiver down her spine. Robert had a criminal record and a history of violence, including multiple instances of assault and a connection to an organized crime syndicate.

The pieces of the puzzle began to fall into place. Robert's encounter with Lily on the night of the murder had been fueled by jealousy and rage, a culmination of his resentment toward Emily's relationship with Lily. It was a motive born out of possessiveness and hatred, a toxic cocktail that had led to a horrifying act of violence.

As Detective Reynolds recounted the events leading up to the tragedy, Jennifer felt a surge of anger and disbelief. How could one person's twisted emotions lead to such a devastating outcome? The weight of the truth was heavy, and yet Jennifer knew that facing it head-on was the only way to honor her mother's memory.

The investigation had unearthed additional evidence – a trail of communications between Robert and an unknown accomplice.

Jennifer's determination to uncover the truth had led her to a network of individuals who had played a role in orchestrating the crime. It was a web of deceit and malevolence, and Jennifer was determined to see justice served.

With Detective Reynolds as her ally, Jennifer delved deeper into the criminal underworld that had played a part in her mother's murder. She tirelessly pursued leads, scrutinized phone records, and collaborated with law enforcement to bring the truth to light. It was a harrowing journey, marked by moments of despair and fleeting glimpses of hope.

One day, as Jennifer sifted through a stack of documents, she stumbled upon a piece of information that sent shockwaves through her. The unknown accomplice had been identified – a man named Victor Russo, a known associate of Robert's criminal connections. The revelation was a chilling reminder of the darkness that had infiltrated her mother's life.

With Detective Reynolds by her side, Jennifer orchestrated a meticulously planned operation to apprehend both Robert Davis and Victor Russo. The stakes were high, the risks even higher, but Jennifer's unwavering determination and the support of her newfound allies propelled her forward.

The day of the operation arrived, and tension hung in the air as law enforcement moved in to apprehend the suspects. The operation was a success, and Jennifer watched as Robert Davis and Victor Russo were led away in handcuffs – a bittersweet victory that brought a sense of closure and justice to her mother's memory.

In the aftermath of the operation, Jennifer stood before her mother's grave, a mixture of emotions coursing through her. The journey had been marked by pain, resilience, and the relentless pursuit of truth. As she whispered her final farewell to her mother, Jennifer knew that her quest for justice had been a testament to the love they shared – a love that had given her the strength to face the darkest corners of the human experience and emerge with a renewed sense of purpose.

The truth had been unveiled, the shadows of uncertainty dispelled. Jennifer's journey had been one of confronting her deepest fears, and as she stood before the gravestone, she felt a profound sense of closure. The memory of her mother would forever be etched in her heart, a guiding light that had led her through the darkness to a place of empowerment and triumph.

Chapter 11: A Mother's Legacy

In the aftermath of her mother's tragic murder and the pursuit of justice that followed, Jennifer found herself drawn to a different aspect of her mother's life – the dreams and aspirations that had shaped Emily's journey. As Jennifer delved into her mother's past, she discovered a world of hopes, passions, and unfulfilled ambitions that added new layers to her understanding of the woman who had raised her.

One afternoon, Jennifer sat in her mother's old study, surrounded by shelves of books and mementos that had once been a cherished part of Emily's life. As Jennifer pored over old journals and handwritten notes, a portrait of her mother's dreams began to emerge.

Emily had harbored a deep love for literature and storytelling. She had dreamed of becoming a published author, penning tales that would capture the imaginations of readers around the world. The study, with its walls lined with books and shelves filled with notebooks, was a testament to her creative spirit.

Jennifer's heart swelled with pride as she read passages from her mother's writings. The words on the pages seemed to come alive, carrying traces of Emily's passion and dedication. Jennifer marveled at her mother's talent, feeling a sense of connection that transcended time and space.

Another discovery awaited Jennifer in a box of old photographs. She found images of her mother participating in charity events, volunteering at community organizations, and engaging in advocacy work. Emily had been deeply committed to making a positive impact on the world around her, using her voice and energy to uplift those in need.

One photograph depicted Emily standing alongside a group of individuals at a local shelter, her smile radiating warmth and compassion. The image spoke volumes about Emily's dedication to service and her belief in the importance of giving back. Jennifer felt a renewed sense of admiration for her mother's selflessness.

As Jennifer continued to unearth her mother's aspirations, she came across a collection of sketches and drawings. Emily had possessed a talent for visual art, capturing the beauty of the world around her with pencil and paper. Each stroke of the pencil seemed to reflect Emily's keen eye and artistic sensibility.

Jennifer's exploration of her mother's legacy extended beyond the confines of their home. She reached out to friends, colleagues, and individuals who had crossed paths with Emily throughout her life. Their stories painted a vivid portrait of a woman who had left an indelible mark on those around her – a mentor, a friend, and a source of inspiration.

One day, Jennifer received a letter from Lily, her mother's close friend. In it, Lily shared anecdotes and memories that spoke to the depth of Emily's character. She recounted their shared dreams, the laughter they had shared, and the unwavering bond that had sustained them through life's challenges.

The letter concluded with a heartfelt sentiment: "Your mother's legacy lives on, Jennifer. She was a beacon of love, resilience, and creativity. As you navigate your own journey, remember that her spirit is a part of you, guiding you toward your own triumphs."

Moved by Lily's words, Jennifer felt a renewed sense of purpose. She had uncovered her mother's dreams, aspirations, and the impact she had made on the world. Emily's legacy was one of love, compassion, and a relentless pursuit of the things that brought her joy and fulfillment.

With a heart full of gratitude, Jennifer embarked on her own path, carrying her mother's legacy as a guiding light. She knew that as she faced the challenges and triumphs that lay ahead, Emily's spirit would be by her side, a constant reminder of the strength and resilience that ran through their veins. And as Jennifer continued to honor her mother's memory, she was determined to create a legacy of her own – one marked by courage, compassion, and the unwavering pursuit of dreams.

Chapter 12: Path to Revenge

The passage of time had done little to quell the storm of emotions that raged within Jennifer's heart. Despite the closure brought about by the arrest and conviction of her mother's murderers, a lingering sense of anger and injustice remained. As Jennifer grappled with her grief, a new emotion began to take root – the gnawing desire for revenge.

The trial had been a painful ordeal, marked by gut-wrenching testimony and harrowing details. Jennifer had faced her mother's killers in court, her eyes locking with theirs as they were held accountable for their actions. While justice had been served, Jennifer couldn't shake the feeling that it was not enough. The wounds ran deep, and the ache for retribution burned within her.

Late one evening, as Jennifer sat alone in her room, her thoughts turned to vengeance. The darkness outside mirrored the tumultuous emotions within her. She began to contemplate the possibility of seeking her own form of justice – a way to make those responsible for her mother's death suffer as she had suffered.

As the idea took hold, Jennifer's mind became consumed by a growing obsession. She began to research the individuals involved in her mother's murder, delving into their pasts and connections. She meticulously pieced together a web of associations, determined to uncover any lingering threads that might lead her to those who had orchestrated the crime.

Jennifer's research led her down a dangerous path, one fraught with risk and moral ambiguity. She considered reaching out to individuals who had ties to the criminal underworld, seeking information that might help her enact her plan for revenge. Her heart raced as she contemplated the steps she might take, each scenario more perilous than the last.

However, a glimmer of reason and sanity remained within Jennifer. It was a voice of caution that whispered against the allure of revenge, reminding her of the darkness it could unleash. She thought of her mother – the woman who had taught her the values of love, compassion, and resilience. She knew that seeking revenge would betray her mother's legacy.

In a moment of clarity, Jennifer reached out to Lily, the friend who had shared a deep connection with her mother. Lily's voice on the other end of the phone was a lifeline, grounding Jennifer in the midst of her tumultuous thoughts.

"Jennifer, revenge is a path that will lead you down a dark and treacherous road," Lily cautioned. "It won't bring your mother back, and it won't heal the wounds within you. The cycle of violence will only perpetuate more pain."

Lily's words struck a chord within Jennifer. She realized that her desire for revenge was a manifestation of her grief – a way to channel the anger and helplessness she felt. Lily reminded her that seeking justice through legal means had already been achieved, and that embracing the path of vengeance would only perpetuate a cycle of pain.

In the days that followed, Jennifer's resolve began to shift. She turned her focus toward healing, seeking solace in therapy, support groups, and the memories of her mother's love. She channeled her energy into advocacy and community service, using her experiences to raise awareness about the impact of violence on families and the importance of seeking healthier paths to healing.

As Jennifer looked to the future, she knew that the desire for revenge would always linger, a shadow that occasionally resurfaced. But she also recognized the strength she had within her – the strength to choose a different path, one that honored her mother's legacy and embraced the values she had instilled.

The journey toward healing was a complex one, marked by moments of struggle and triumph. And as Jennifer navigated the twists and turns of her emotions, she held onto the lessons her mother had taught her – the power of love, the importance of resilience, and the enduring strength that resided within her. In choosing the path of healing over revenge, Jennifer began to forge her own legacy – one of courage, compassion, and the unwavering pursuit of a brighter

Chapter 13: Legal Battles

In the wake of the trial that had brought justice for her mother's murder, Jennifer's desire for closure was met with a new set of challenges – the legal battles that unfolded in the aftermath. As she navigated the complexities of the legal system, Jennifer discovered that the pursuit of justice was far from straightforward.

The courtroom had been a battlefield, a place where evidence was presented, witnesses testified, and emotions ran high. Jennifer had witnessed the culmination of her mother's case, and while the verdict had brought a sense of vindication, the aftermath introduced a new set of obstacles.

Days turned into weeks as Jennifer met with lawyers, reviewed documents, and navigated the labyrinthine world of legal proceedings. The trial had ended, but the legal battles were far from over. The process of seeking restitution for her mother's death was a complex endeavor, one that required patience, persistence, and a willingness to confront the bureaucratic intricacies of the system.

Jennifer's journey led her to meetings with lawyers who specialized in victims' rights and restitution. She learned about the intricacies of civil lawsuits, the challenges of obtaining compensation, and the lengthy process of navigating the legal landscape. The pursuit of justice was a marathon, not a sprint, and Jennifer's determination was put to the test.

As she delved deeper into the legal battles, Jennifer began to encounter roadblocks that tested her resolve. Bureaucratic red tape, delays, and conflicting interests created a frustrating landscape that seemed to impede progress at every turn. The realization that justice was not as swift or straightforward as she had hoped was a sobering one.

One particular meeting with a lawyer named Sarah Parker shed light on the complexities of seeking restitution. Sarah, a seasoned advocate for victims' rights, explained the nuances of the process and the uphill battle that lay ahead.

"Jennifer, seeking restitution is a challenging endeavor," Sarah began, her tone empathetic. "While the criminal trial brought accountability, the road to financial compensation can be arduous. The legal system is often ill-equipped to provide swift and comprehensive remedies."

Jennifer listened as Sarah explained the hurdles – the need to prove damages, the limited resources of the court, and the potential for appeals that could further prolong the process. It was a disheartening reality, one that highlighted the disparities between the criminal justice system and the pursuit of financial restitution.

As Jennifer absorbed the information, a mix of frustration and determination welled within her. She was faced with a stark choice – to continue navigating the legal battles with the understanding that the road ahead would be long and uncertain, or to shift her focus toward other forms of healing and advocacy.

Sarah's words resonated with Jennifer, echoing in her mind long after the meeting had concluded. The pursuit of justice, it seemed, was a multifaceted endeavor that required both legal action and a commitment to raising awareness, advocating for change, and supporting others who had experienced similar losses.

In the days that followed, Jennifer made a decision. She would continue her legal battle, determined to secure financial restitution for her mother's death. But she would also channel her energy into broader advocacy efforts – using her experience to shed light on the challenges faced by victims within the legal system and advocating for reforms that would streamline the process.

As Jennifer walked the path of legal battles, she did so with a renewed sense of purpose. The road ahead was uncertain, marked by challenges and obstacles. But Jennifer's determination remained unwavering, fueled by the memory of her mother's resilience and the belief that her pursuit of justice could spark meaningful change – not just for herself, but for countless others who had walked a similar path of pain and perseverance.

Chapter 14: The Power of Forgiveness

In the wake of the legal battles and the pursuit of justice for her mother's murder, Jennifer found herself grappling with a complex and tumultuous emotion – forgiveness. As she stared at the faces of the perpetrators during the trial, Jennifer was confronted with a moral dilemma that would test the boundaries of her compassion and humanity.

The courtroom had been a place of confrontation, a battlefield where evidence clashed and emotions ran high. Jennifer had seen the individuals responsible for her mother's death – their faces etched with a mixture of guilt and defiance. As the verdict was read, a sense of closure had washed over her, but it was accompanied by an unexpected surge of conflicting emotions.

In the days that followed, Jennifer's thoughts turned to the concept of forgiveness. The idea seemed foreign, almost counterintuitive, given the magnitude of the crime that had been committed. And yet, a part of Jennifer recognized that forgiveness might hold the key to her own healing and liberation.

As Jennifer sat in therapy, she began to explore her feelings towards the perpetrators. She grappled with the rage that had simmered beneath the surface – a fire fueled by the pain of her mother's absence. And yet, she also began to glimpse the possibility of forgiveness as a transformative force – one that could release her from the chains of anger and resentment.

Her therapist, Dr. Hernandez, guided her through the complex terrain of forgiveness. "Forgiveness doesn't mean condoning or excusing their actions," Dr. Hernandez explained gently. "It's about releasing the power they hold over your emotions and finding peace within yourself."

Jennifer listened intently, her heart torn between the desire for justice and the yearning for inner peace. She began to reflect on her mother's legacy – the values of love, compassion, and resilience that had been instilled in her from a young age. Could she find it within herself to embody those values, even in the face of such profound tragedy?

The journey towards forgiveness was a rocky one, marked by moments of doubt and introspection. Jennifer found herself wrestling with questions that had no easy answers. Could she forgive those who had taken her mother's life? Could she find a way to let go of the anger that had consumed her for so long?

One day, as Jennifer visited her mother's grave, she found herself speaking aloud, her voice carrying the weight of her emotions. "Mom, I don't know if I can ever truly forgive them for what they did," she whispered, tears streaming down her face. "But I want to try. I want to find a way to free myself from this anger and pain."

In the weeks that followed, Jennifer embarked on a journey of introspection and self-discovery. She began to practice mindfulness and meditation, seeking moments of stillness that allowed her to confront the turbulent sea of emotions within her. She reached out to a support group for survivors of violent crime, finding solace in the shared experiences and stories of forgiveness.

Slowly but surely, Jennifer's heart began to soften. She found herself reflecting on the human complexities that had led the perpetrators down their destructive path. She acknowledged the pain and brokenness that might have fueled their actions, even as she condemned their choices.

In a poignant moment of clarity, Jennifer penned a letter to the perpetrators. In it, she expressed her pain, her anger, and her struggle to forgive. She acknowledged the profound impact of their actions on her life and the void that her mother's absence had left behind. And yet, she also extended a glimmer of empathy, recognizing the potential for redemption and transformation.

The act of writing the letter was cathartic – a release of emotions that had long been held captive within her. And as Jennifer sealed the envelope, she felt a sense of closure, a realization that forgiveness was not a single, defining moment, but a journey that unfolded over time.

As Jennifer's heart gradually embraced the concept of forgiveness, she found a measure of peace that had eluded her for so long. The anger did not disappear entirely, but it no longer held her in its grip. Instead, Jennifer discovered a newfound strength – the power to transcend the cycle of pain and find healing within herself.

The path to forgiveness was a testament to Jennifer's resilience and the enduring legacy of her mother's love. It was a journey that transformed her, allowing her to reclaim her own narrative and find solace in the transformative power of compassion. And as Jennifer walked the road towards forgiveness, she carried her mother's spirit with her, a guiding light that illuminated the path towards inner freedom and the unwavering pursuit of a life lived with purpose and grace.

Chapter 15: Discovering Finance

In the midst of her journey towards healing and self-discovery, Jennifer found an unexpected avenue through which to channel her energy – the world of business and finance. As she embarked on a path of empowerment and growth, Jennifer's interest in this new realm began to flourish, opening doors to a future she had never anticipated.

It was during a chance encounter with a financial article that Jennifer's curiosity was piqued. The intricate dance of numbers and the concept of strategic decision-making captured her attention. The more she delved into the world of finance, the more she realized its potential as a powerful tool for creating change and achieving her goals.

Jennifer's interest led her to enroll in introductory business and finance courses at a local community college. The journey was a challenging one, marked by late nights of studying, stacks of textbooks, and the unwavering determination to absorb as much knowledge as possible. Jennifer's drive to succeed was fueled by a desire to honor her mother's memory and forge a path towards a brighter future.

As the semesters passed, Jennifer's understanding of finance deepened. The once-daunting concepts of budgeting, investment, and risk management became familiar territory. Jennifer's analytical mind thrived in the world of spreadsheets and financial calculations, and she discovered a newfound sense of purpose in the pursuit of financial literacy.

Jennifer's passion for finance also found a creative outlet in her artwork. She began to merge her love for painting with her newfound interest, creating intricate visual representations of economic principles and market dynamics. Her artwork became a reflection of her evolving journey, a testament to the fusion of creativity and logic that defined her approach to business and finance.

Outside of the classroom, Jennifer sought opportunities to gain practical experience. She interned at a local financial firm, where she absorbed insights from seasoned professionals and witnessed firsthand the impact of financial decisions on individuals and businesses. The exposure was invaluable, offering a glimpse into the real-world applications of the concepts she had been studying.

Amidst her academic pursuits and professional endeavors, Jennifer's path intersected with a mentor named Sarah Mitchell. Sarah, a successful entrepreneur and finance expert, recognized Jennifer's potential and took her under her wing. Their conversations were a wellspring of wisdom and guidance, as Sarah shared her experiences, insights, and lessons learned on her own journey.

"Jennifer, finance is more than just numbers – it's about understanding the dynamics of money and using that knowledge to shape your future," Sarah advised. "Whether you're managing your own finances or making strategic decisions for a business, the principles remain the same. It's a powerful tool for creating positive change."

Sarah's words resonated deeply with Jennifer, igniting a fire within her. She realized that her interest in finance was not just a personal pursuit, but a means to effect meaningful change – a way to honor her mother's legacy by making informed decisions that could positively impact her life and the lives of others.

As Jennifer continued to immerse herself in the world of business and finance, she discovered a profound sense of empowerment. The once-unfamiliar terrain had become a realm of possibility, a canvas upon which she could paint a future of her own design. Jennifer's journey was marked by resilience, courage, and the unwavering pursuit of knowledge – qualities that mirrored the spirit of her mother and the legacy of love and strength that had been passed down to her.

With each step forward, Jennifer's interest in business and finance grew, propelling her towards a future that held limitless potential. And as she stood on the precipice of new opportunities, she carried her mother's memory in her heart, a guiding force that fueled her determination to forge a path of empowerment, impact, and the fulfillment of dreams yet to be realized.

Chapter 16: Mentorship

Jennifer's journey into the world of business and finance led her to unexpected places, and one of the most transformative stops along the way was the discovery of a mentor – a successful businesswoman named Elizabeth Turner.

Jennifer had first encountered Elizabeth during a guest lecture at her college. Elizabeth's commanding presence and insightful perspectives had captured Jennifer's attention, and she was eager to learn more. After the lecture, Jennifer approached Elizabeth, expressing her admiration for her achievements and her desire to learn from her.

Impressed by Jennifer's enthusiasm and determination, Elizabeth agreed to become her mentor. Their mentorship journey began with a casual coffee meeting, during which Jennifer shared her aspirations and the path that had led her to the world of business and finance. Elizabeth, in turn, shared her own journey – the challenges she had faced, the lessons she had learned, and the principles that had guided her success.

"Jennifer, mentorship is about more than just sharing knowledge – it's about fostering growth, supporting one another, and learning from each other's experiences," Elizabeth explained. "I believe in paying it forward and helping the next generation of leaders reach their full potential."

Under Elizabeth's guidance, Jennifer's understanding of business and finance deepened. Their discussions covered a wide range of topics, from investment strategies and market trends to leadership principles and effective communication. Jennifer soaked up every piece of advice, recognizing the invaluable opportunity to learn from someone who had walked the path she aspired to tread.

Beyond the technical aspects, Elizabeth also imparted invaluable life lessons. She emphasized the importance of resilience in the face of challenges, the value of cultivating a growth mindset, and the significance of building strong relationships in the business world.

As their mentorship flourished, Jennifer's confidence grew. She began to apply the insights she had gained to her coursework, internships, and personal projects. Elizabeth's guidance became a touchstone, guiding Jennifer through tough decisions and moments of uncertainty.

One day, as Jennifer and Elizabeth sat in a park, Jennifer broached a topic that had been weighing on her mind. "Elizabeth, I've been considering starting my own business – a venture that aligns with my passion for finance and my desire to make a positive impact. But I'm nervous about taking that leap."

Elizabeth smiled warmly, her eyes reflecting a mix of empathy and encouragement. "Jennifer, entrepreneurship is both exhilarating and challenging. It requires courage, determination, and a willingness to embrace the unknown. But I believe in you, and I'm here to support you every step of the way."

Inspired by Elizabeth's words, Jennifer embarked on the journey of entrepreneurship. With Elizabeth as her mentor, she navigated the complexities of business planning, financial projections, and market analysis. The process was marked by moments of excitement and moments of doubt, but Jennifer's unwavering determination and the guidance of her mentor propelled her forward.

As Jennifer's business began to take shape, Elizabeth's support remained a constant presence. She offered advice on strategic partnerships, provided feedback on business plans, and shared insights from her own experiences as an entrepreneur. Jennifer's appreciation for Elizabeth's mentorship deepened with each passing day.

The mentorship extended beyond business matters. Elizabeth became a source of inspiration and guidance in Jennifer's personal life as well. She encouraged Jennifer to maintain a healthy work-life balance, prioritize self-care, and cultivate a strong sense of purpose.

Months turned into years, and Jennifer's business flourished under Elizabeth's mentorship. The venture became a testament to Jennifer's resilience, creativity, and the invaluable guidance she had received. As she looked back on her journey, Jennifer recognized the profound impact of mentorship – the power of one person's wisdom and support to shape the trajectory of another's life.

Their mentorship had been a transformative chapter in Jennifer's journey – a chapter marked by growth, empowerment, and the unwavering belief in the potential of a young woman with a dream. And as Jennifer continued to forge her path in the world of business and finance, she carried with her the lessons, insights, and friendship that had been nurtured through the powerful bond of mentorship.

Chapter 17: Educational Pursuits

Jennifer's dedication to her studies and her passion for business and finance began to bear fruit in ways she had never imagined. As she poured herself into her education, her unwavering commitment and thirst for knowledge led to remarkable achievements and opportunities.

The hallways of her college became a familiar landscape as Jennifer pursued her degree in finance. She immersed herself in coursework, engaging in lively discussions, and absorbing insights from professors and peers alike. Her diligence and enthusiasm for learning set her apart, earning her the respect and admiration of her professors.

As her academic journey progressed, Jennifer's grades soared. She consistently excelled in her classes, earning top marks and recognition for her achievements. Her determination was fueled by a desire to honor her mother's memory and to pave the way for a future that held the promise of empowerment and impact.

Jennifer's exceptional academic performance did not go unnoticed. She was awarded scholarships and honors, each accolade a testament to her hard work and dedication. The financial support she received eased the burden of tuition and allowed her to fully invest herself in her studies and extracurricular pursuits.

One day, Jennifer received a letter that would change the trajectory of her educational journey – an invitation to join an exclusive honors program. The program offered a unique blend of academic rigor, leadership development, and mentorship opportunities. It was a chance for Jennifer to further elevate her education and expand her horizons.

As part of the honors program, Jennifer found herself surrounded by a community of driven and ambitious individuals. The program's curriculum challenged her to think critically, solve complex problems, and engage in projects that had real-world impact. Jennifer's thirst for knowledge and her determination to make a difference found a perfect outlet within the program's framework.

One of the highlights of the honors program was the opportunity for experiential learning. Jennifer participated in internships, research projects, and community engagement initiatives that allowed her to apply her classroom knowledge to practical scenarios. The experience broadened her perspective, deepened her understanding of finance's real-world applications, and further fueled her passion.

Jennifer's dedication to her education was not limited to her own growth. She recognized the importance of giving back and paying it forward. As part of the honors program, she became a mentor to underclassmen, offering guidance, support, and insights gleaned from her own journey. Jennifer's role as a mentor allowed her to inspire and empower others, fostering a sense of community and shared aspiration.

Amidst her studies and mentorship efforts, Jennifer's business endeavors continued to flourish. The venture she had embarked upon with Elizabeth's guidance gained traction, earning recognition and accolades within the industry. Jennifer's unique blend of creativity, analytical acumen, and unwavering dedication set her business apart, positioning her as a rising star in the world of finance.

As Jennifer's college years drew to a close, she reflected on the remarkable journey she had undertaken. Her path had been marked by resilience, passion, and an unyielding commitment to her dreams. The challenges she had faced had only fueled her determination, and the support she had received had nurtured her growth.

With her degree in hand and a future brimming with potential, Jennifer stood at the threshold of a new chapter. The pursuit of education had been a transformative force, empowering her to create change, inspire others, and forge a path of impact. And as she ventured forth, Jennifer carried with her the legacy of her mother's love, the wisdom of her mentor, and the unwavering belief in the boundless possibilities that lay ahead.

Chapter 18: University Life

The bustling campus of Eastwood University welcomed Jennifer with a sense of anticipation and excitement as she embarked on a new chapter of her life. Armed with a passion for business and finance, Jennifer was determined to make the most of her university experience and forge a path toward her dreams.

Orientation week buzzed with activity, and Jennifer eagerly attended seminars, workshops, and networking events. The vibrant atmosphere ignited her enthusiasm and deepened her sense of purpose. As she connected with fellow students who shared her interests, Jennifer felt a sense of camaraderie that bolstered her resolve.

The first day of classes marked the beginning of Jennifer's academic journey. Her schedule was a mix of foundational business courses, finance theory, and quantitative analysis. The challenges were formidable, but Jennifer's determination was unwavering. She immersed herself in her studies, dedicating countless hours to lectures, readings, and assignments.

In the lecture halls and discussion groups, Jennifer's passion for the subject matter was palpable. She engaged in lively debates, posed thoughtful questions, and collaborated with her peers on group projects. Her commitment to excellence and her thirst for knowledge set the tone for her university experience.

Outside of the classroom, Jennifer sought to broaden her horizons through extracurricular activities. She joined business and finance clubs, participated in case competitions, and attended guest lectures by industry professionals. Each opportunity provided a platform for Jennifer to apply her learning in real-world scenarios, gaining insights that transcended textbooks.

One day, as Jennifer perused a bulletin board on campus, a flyer caught her eye. It advertised an upcoming entrepreneurship conference, featuring speakers who had achieved success in various industries. Eager to learn from accomplished entrepreneurs, Jennifer registered for the event and eagerly anticipated the insights she would gain.

The entrepreneurship conference proved to be a turning point for Jennifer. Listening to the speakers' stories of resilience, innovation, and the pursuit of dreams ignited a fire within her. The idea of starting her own business began to take root, fueled by the belief that she could make a meaningful impact in the world of finance.

Inspired by the conference, Jennifer sought guidance from her professors, tapping into their wealth of knowledge and experience. She also reached out to local entrepreneurs, conducting informational interviews and seeking insights into the challenges and rewards of starting a business. The conversations deepened her understanding and stoked her entrepreneurial spirit.

Amidst the academic rigor and extracurricular pursuits, Jennifer's personal growth was profound. University life became a crucible for self-discovery, resilience, and the cultivation of essential life skills. She learned to manage her time effectively, navigate complex challenges, and embrace the value of collaboration and diverse perspectives.

As Jennifer's first semester came to a close, she reflected on the transformative journey she had undertaken. Her university experience had been a whirlwind of learning, growth, and the pursuit of her passions. Armed with newfound knowledge and a vision for the future, Jennifer looked ahead with a sense of determination and anticipation, ready to embrace the opportunities that lay ahead on her path in business and finance.

Chapter 19: First Taste of Entrepreneurship

The seed of entrepreneurship that had been planted within Jennifer continued to grow as she navigated her business and finance studies at Eastwood University. Eager to put her knowledge into action, Jennifer embarked on a journey that would lead her to her first taste of entrepreneurship – launching a small online venture.

The idea had been brewing in Jennifer's mind for months, a fusion of her passion for finance and her desire to create a positive impact. Inspired by her mentor Elizabeth's guidance and her own experiences, Jennifer envisioned an online platform that would provide financial education and resources to individuals seeking to improve their financial literacy.

With determination in her heart and a clear vision in mind, Jennifer set to work. She spent late nights brainstorming, researching, and sketching out the concept for her platform. The process was both exhilarating and daunting, but Jennifer's unwavering commitment fueled her progress.

After weeks of planning, Jennifer unveiled her creation – "Financial Foundations," an interactive online hub designed to demystify financial concepts, provide practical tips, and empower individuals to take control of their financial well-being. The platform featured blog articles, infographics, and interactive tools that catered to a wide range of audiences.

The launch of "Financial Foundations" was met with enthusiasm. Jennifer's dedication to providing valuable content and her genuine desire to make a difference resonated with users. The platform's user base began to grow, and positive feedback poured in, affirming Jennifer's belief in the importance of financial education.

As Jennifer's online venture gained momentum, she found herself juggling the demands of entrepreneurship with her academic commitments. Late nights were spent crafting content, engaging with users, and fine-tuning the platform's user experience. Despite the challenges, Jennifer's passion and sense of purpose fueled her determination to see her vision through.

One day, Jennifer received an unexpected email from a reader named Alex. Alex shared how "Financial Foundations" had transformed her perspective on money management and inspired her to take proactive steps towards her financial goals. The message was a poignant reminder of the impact Jennifer's venture was having on individuals' lives.

The success of "Financial Foundations" also caught the attention of the university's entrepreneurship center. Jennifer was invited to participate in a startup accelerator program, which provided mentorship, resources, and networking opportunities to budding entrepreneurs. The experience exposed Jennifer to a community of like-minded innovators and offered her insights into the intricacies of business development.

As Jennifer's small online venture continued to thrive, she began to envision new possibilities for growth. She expanded the platform's offerings, collaborating with finance experts to host webinars, workshops, and virtual events. The platform's reach extended beyond the university, attracting users from diverse backgrounds who shared a common goal of improving their financial literacy.

The journey of entrepreneurship was marked by highs and lows, moments of exhilaration and moments of doubt. But through it all, Jennifer's resilience and unwavering commitment propelled her forward. She recognized that her venture was not just a business endeavor – it was a manifestation of her values, a channel for impact, and a testament to the transformative power of pursuing one's passions.

As Jennifer looked back on the evolution of "Financial Foundations," she marveled at the path she had undertaken. The small online venture had become a symbol of her entrepreneurial spirit, her dedication to financial education, and her belief in the potential of individuals to achieve financial empowerment.

And as Jennifer continued to navigate the complex landscape of entrepreneurship, she carried with her the invaluable lessons learned – the importance of resilience, the value of community, and the unwavering belief in the boundless possibilities that could be unlocked through the pursuit of dreams.

Chapter 20: Overcoming Challenges

Jennifer's journey of entrepreneurship was not without its share of challenges. As she navigated the dynamic landscape of launching and growing her online platform, "Financial Foundations," she encountered obstacles that tested her resilience, creativity, and determination.

The initial excitement of launching "Financial Foundations" had given way to the reality of the entrepreneurial journey. Jennifer faced the daunting task of balancing her academic commitments, managing the platform's content, and engaging with users. The demands were immense, and Jennifer found herself grappling with time constraints and competing priorities.

One of the first challenges Jennifer encountered was the need to continuously generate valuable and engaging content for her platform. The pressure to produce high-quality articles, infographics, and interactive tools while maintaining a rigorous academic schedule took a toll on her. There were moments when she felt overwhelmed and wondered if she could sustain the momentum.

During a particularly challenging period, Jennifer turned to her mentor, Elizabeth, for guidance. Elizabeth reminded Jennifer of the importance of pacing herself, setting realistic expectations, and seeking support when needed. "Jennifer, remember that challenges are a natural part of the entrepreneurial journey," Elizabeth advised. "It's okay to ask for help and take breaks when necessary. Your journey is a marathon, not a sprint."

The wisdom of Elizabeth's words resonated with Jennifer. She began to delegate certain tasks to a small team of dedicated volunteers who shared her passion for financial education. The collaborative effort breathed new life into "Financial Foundations," allowing Jennifer to focus on strategic planning and user engagement.

However, as "Financial Foundations" gained popularity, Jennifer encountered another hurdle – financial sustainability. The platform required resources for web hosting, marketing, and technology upgrades. Jennifer's determination to provide free and accessible financial education clashed with the financial realities of running a venture.

Jennifer faced a difficult decision – whether to introduce subscription-based models, advertisements, or seek external funding. The ethical dilemma weighed heavily on her. She didn't want to compromise the platform's mission, but she also recognized the need for financial stability to ensure its longevity.

In search of guidance, Jennifer attended a panel discussion on ethical entrepreneurship. Listening to experienced entrepreneurs share their insights, she realized that the pursuit of social impact and financial sustainability were not mutually exclusive. Jennifer learned that seeking financial viability could enable her to expand her reach and make an even greater impact.

With newfound clarity, Jennifer decided to introduce a tiered subscription model for "Financial Foundations." She ensured that a portion of the proceeds would be reinvested into creating free resources for underserved communities. The decision was met with mixed reactions from users, but Jennifer's transparency and commitment to her mission resonated with many.

The challenges Jennifer faced became opportunities for growth and learning. They taught her the importance of adaptability, strategic decision-making, and the value of seeking guidance from mentors and peers. Through each setback, Jennifer developed a deeper understanding of the intricate dance between passion and practicality in the world of entrepreneurship.

As Jennifer navigated the stormy waters of setbacks and challenges, she emerged stronger and more resolute. The path of entrepreneurship was not a linear one, but a journey marked by twists, turns, and unexpected detours. Jennifer's ability to overcome obstacles and stay true to her vision was a testament to her resilience and her unyielding commitment to making a positive impact through "Financial Foundations."

And as Jennifer continued to navigate the complex landscape of entrepreneurship, she carried with her the invaluable lessons learned – the importance of adaptability, the power of community, and the unwavering belief in the transformative potential of perseverance and passion.

Chapter 21: Networking and Connections

In the ever-evolving world of business and finance, Jennifer came to understand the significance of networking and building meaningful connections. As her entrepreneurial journey continued and her aspirations expanded, Jennifer recognized that the power of relationships could open doors, foster growth, and amplify her impact.

Attending conferences, workshops, and industry events became an integral part of Jennifer's routine. These gatherings offered opportunities to connect with fellow entrepreneurs, finance professionals, and thought leaders. Jennifer's genuine curiosity, enthusiasm, and willingness to learn set the stage for authentic interactions that transcended superficial networking.

One such event was the Annual Finance Summit, a prestigious gathering of finance experts and innovators. Jennifer eagerly registered, excited by the prospect of learning from industry pioneers and expanding her professional circle. Little did she know that the summit would be a catalyst for new opportunities and connections that would shape her journey.

During a breakout session on fintech innovation, Jennifer found herself engaged in a conversation with a fellow attendee named Marcus Reynolds. Marcus was the founder of a successful fintech startup that aimed to democratize access to financial services. Intrigued by Jennifer's passion for financial education and her online platform, Marcus expressed interest in collaborating on a project.

The connection with Marcus marked the beginning of a transformative partnership. Over the following months, Jennifer and Marcus worked closely to develop a series of webinars and workshops that merged the worlds of financial technology and education. The collaboration leveraged Jennifer's expertise in financial literacy and Marcus's fintech insights to create engaging and informative content.

As the partnership flourished, Jennifer's professional circle expanded further. She was introduced to mentors, advisors, and industry experts who provided guidance, insights, and opportunities for growth. Jennifer attended roundtable discussions, participated in mentorship programs, and sought out conversations with individuals who had achieved success in various corners of the business and finance world.

One day, Jennifer received an invitation to join a prestigious network of young entrepreneurs and change-makers. The network provided a platform for collaboration, knowledge exchange, and access to resources that could accelerate Jennifer's ventures. The acceptance into the network was a validation of her dedication and an acknowledgment of her potential as a future leader.

Amidst the whirlwind of networking events and professional connections, Jennifer remained grounded in her mission. She continued to nurture "Financial Foundations," expanding its reach and impact. The partnerships she had forged enriched the platform's content and offerings, allowing Jennifer to provide even greater value to her users.

One evening, as Jennifer reflected on her journey of networking and connections, she realized that her professional circle had become a tapestry of diverse perspectives, experiences, and expertise. Each connection had enriched her understanding, broadened her horizons, and reaffirmed her belief in the power of collaboration to drive positive change.

Jennifer's journey was a testament to the transformational potential of networking – the art of forging relationships that extend beyond business cards and LinkedIn connections. Her network had become a source of inspiration, support, and mutual growth, fueling her entrepreneurial spirit and empowering her to make a lasting impact in the world of business and finance.

And as Jennifer looked ahead to the opportunities that lay on the horizon, she carried with her the invaluable lessons learned – the importance of authenticity, the power of genuine connections, and the unwavering belief in the boundless possibilities that could be unlocked through the art of networking and the cultivation of meaningful relationships.

Chapter 22: Rising Ambitions

As Jennifer's journey through the world of business and finance continued, her ambitions soared to new heights. The experiences, lessons, and connections she had accumulated fueled her desire to take on an even greater challenge – starting her own business.

The seed of this ambition had been planted long ago, nurtured by Jennifer's mother's unwavering belief in her potential and her mentor Elizabeth's guidance. With each step along her path – from launching "Financial Foundations" to collaborating on innovative projects – Jennifer's confidence in her ability to make a lasting impact grew stronger.

It was on a clear spring morning, as Jennifer sat in a coffee shop with her notebook and a steaming cup of tea, that the idea for her own business venture crystallized. Inspired by her experiences and the gaps she had identified in the financial industry, Jennifer envisioned a consultancy that would empower individuals and businesses to make informed financial decisions.

The vision for her consultancy was clear – a holistic approach that blended financial education, strategic planning, and personalized guidance. Jennifer envisioned a platform where individuals could access resources, attend workshops, and receive one-on-one coaching to achieve their financial goals.

Excitement bubbled within Jennifer as she sketched out the blueprint for her consultancy. She thought about the impact it could have – helping individuals break free from financial constraints, guiding businesses towards sustainable growth, and fostering a culture of financial empowerment.

However, as Jennifer delved deeper into the details of her business plan, she encountered challenges that tested her resolve. The prospect of launching a consultancy from scratch was daunting. Jennifer grappled with questions about funding, market positioning, and how to effectively communicate the value of her services.

Doubts crept in, and Jennifer found herself seeking solace in her mentor's wisdom. Elizabeth listened attentively as Jennifer poured out her concerns and fears. With a reassuring smile, Elizabeth reminded Jennifer of the obstacles she had overcome and the lessons she had learned. "Jennifer, remember that every successful venture starts with a dream and a leap of faith," Elizabeth advised. "Your passion, knowledge, and determination will carry you through the challenges."

With renewed determination, Jennifer dove back into her business plan. She sought guidance from her professional network, tapping into the expertise of mentors and peers who had embarked on similar journeys. The support she received was overwhelming – individuals offered insights, feedback, and even connections to potential partners and investors.

As Jennifer's vision took shape, she began to assemble a team of individuals who shared her passion and belief in the power of financial empowerment. Each member brought a unique set of skills and perspectives, contributing to the foundation of the consultancy. The camaraderie and shared sense of purpose fueled Jennifer's drive to bring her dream to fruition.

Months of meticulous planning, late nights, and iterative refinement culminated in a defining moment – the official launch of Jennifer's consultancy, "Empower Finance." The platform went live, offering a range of services that catered to individuals, families, and businesses. The response was overwhelmingly positive, with clients expressing gratitude for the guidance and support they received.

As "Empower Finance" gained momentum, Jennifer marveled at the journey she had undertaken. The challenges she had faced had only served to strengthen her resolve and deepen her appreciation for the transformative potential of entrepreneurship. Through her consultancy, Jennifer was not only fulfilling her dream of business ownership, but also paying homage to her mother's legacy and creating a lasting impact in the world of finance.

And as Jennifer looked ahead to the path that lay before her, she carried with her the lessons learned – the importance of perseverance, the power of a clear vision, and the unwavering belief in the boundless possibilities that could be unlocked through the pursuit of dreams and the courage to turn ambition into reality.

Chapter 23: Startup Ventures

With the launch of "Empower Finance," Jennifer had taken a bold step into the world of entrepreneurship. As her consultancy gained traction and made a meaningful impact on individuals and businesses, Jennifer's appetite for innovation and growth only grew stronger. Encouraged by her early successes, she began to explore new avenues for expansion and launched her first attempts at other startup ventures.

The first venture that Jennifer embarked upon was an online financial literacy course. Drawing on her expertise and passion for educating others, she developed a comprehensive curriculum that covered topics ranging from budgeting and investing to retirement planning and wealth management. The course was designed to provide individuals with practical tools and knowledge to navigate their financial journeys with confidence.

As Jennifer worked tirelessly to create the course content, she faced the challenge of translating complex financial concepts into accessible and engaging lessons. She sought to strike a balance between technical accuracy and user-friendly language, ensuring that the course would resonate with a diverse audience. Late nights were spent scripting videos, designing interactive modules, and crafting assessments that would empower learners to take control of their finances.

The launch of the online financial literacy course was met with anticipation. Jennifer's platform had already established a reputation for providing valuable resources, and the course represented a natural extension of her mission. The response was overwhelmingly positive, with individuals from various backgrounds enrolling to enhance their financial knowledge and skills.

Jennifer's second venture was inspired by the evolving landscape of sustainable finance. She recognized the growing demand for investment opportunities that aligned with environmental, social, and governance (ESG) principles. With a team of experts, Jennifer launched an online platform that facilitated sustainable investing, connecting investors with companies and projects that championed ethical and responsible practices.

The sustainable investing platform posed unique challenges – from sourcing credible ESG data to developing user-friendly tools for portfolio analysis. Jennifer's team worked tirelessly to ensure that the platform provided accurate information, insightful research, and a seamless user experience. The goal was to empower investors to make informed decisions that not only generated financial returns but also contributed to positive social and environmental impact.

As both ventures gained momentum, Jennifer found herself navigating the intricacies of scaling a business. She faced operational challenges, including resource allocation, team management, and ensuring the sustainability of her ventures. Jennifer's ability to lead her teams, make strategic decisions, and adapt to changing circumstances became pivotal in overcoming obstacles and charting a course for growth.

However, the journey was not without its share of setbacks. Jennifer encountered unexpected technical glitches in the online financial literacy course, and the sustainable investing platform faced regulatory hurdles that required careful navigation. These challenges tested Jennifer's resilience and problem-solving skills, prompting her to seek guidance from mentors, advisors, and her professional network.

Jennifer's willingness to learn from setbacks and iterate on her ventures was a testament to her entrepreneurial spirit. Each hurdle she faced became an opportunity for growth and refinement. Through tenacity and collaboration, Jennifer overcame obstacles and continued to steer her ventures towards success.

As Jennifer reflected on her journey of startup ventures, she marveled at the transformation she had undergone. The process of launching and growing businesses had honed her leadership, expanded her skill set, and reinforced her belief in the power of innovation. The ventures she had undertaken were not just business endeavors – they were a manifestation of her dedication to making a positive impact and a testament to the boundless possibilities that could be unlocked through the pursuit of entrepreneurial dreams.

And as Jennifer looked ahead to the future, she carried with her the lessons learned – the importance of adaptability, the value of resilience, and the unwavering belief in the transformative potential of turning ideas into action. Her journey through startup ventures was a testament to her determination to leave a lasting mark on the world of business and finance.

Chapter 24: Learning from Failure

Jennifer's journey through the world of entrepreneurship had been marked by remarkable successes and transformative growth. However, the path of entrepreneurship is rarely without its bumps and setbacks. It was during one of these challenging moments that Jennifer learned one of her most valuable lessons – the art of learning from failure.

Amidst the bustling landscape of startup ventures and business expansion, Jennifer had undertaken a new project – a financial technology app designed to provide users with personalized budgeting and financial planning tools. Fueled by her passion for technology and her commitment to financial empowerment, Jennifer poured her energy into developing a user-friendly, feature-rich app.

Months of hard work culminated in the app's launch. Jennifer's excitement was palpable as she eagerly awaited the response from users. The initial feedback was positive, and the app's user base began to grow steadily. It seemed that Jennifer's newest venture was poised for success.

However, as the weeks went by, Jennifer started to notice a decline in user engagement. The app's retention rate was lower than she had anticipated, and negative reviews began to surface. Jennifer felt a sense of frustration and disappointment – her vision for the app had been ambitious, and the reality was falling short.

Amidst the setbacks, Jennifer's determination and resilience kicked into high gear. She sought to understand the reasons behind the app's underperformance and embarked on a process of rigorous analysis. Feedback from users highlighted various usability issues, feature gaps, and challenges with the app's onboarding process.

The realization that her project had encountered challenges was a tough pill to swallow, but Jennifer recognized that failure was an opportunity for growth. She delved into research, conducted user surveys, and engaged in candid conversations with her team and industry experts. The goal was not to place blame, but to identify areas for improvement and chart a path forward.

The turning point came during a conversation with Marcus, her collaborator from a previous venture. Marcus shared insights from his own experiences with product development and emphasized the importance of iterative refinement. "Jennifer, setbacks are an inevitable part of the journey," Marcus said. "What matters is how you respond – by learning, adapting, and evolving."

Jennifer's setback became a catalyst for transformation. She made the difficult decision to temporarily halt the app's operations and focus on addressing the user concerns. Jennifer worked closely with her team to implement updates, enhance user experience, and streamline the app's features. The process was marked by late nights, intensive testing, and a commitment to delivering a product that truly resonated with users.

Months of tireless effort culminated in a relaunch of the app. This time, Jennifer had taken the lessons learned from failure to heart. The app featured improved usability, a revamped onboarding process, and a suite of new features that addressed user feedback. The response was overwhelmingly positive, and user engagement began to rebound.

Jennifer's experience with the setback had been transformative. She had learned that failure was not an endpoint, but a stepping stone towards growth and improvement. The setbacks had tested her resilience, honed her problem-solving skills, and deepened her appreciation for the iterative nature of entrepreneurship.

As Jennifer reflected on the journey, she recognized that failure was not something to be feared, but a natural part of the entrepreneurial process. The setbacks had taught her the importance of humility, adaptability, and the unwavering belief in her ability to navigate challenges. Through her experience, Jennifer had learned that failure was not a reflection of her worth as an entrepreneur, but an opportunity to evolve, innovate, and create even greater impact in the world of business and finance.

And as Jennifer looked ahead to the future, she carried with her the invaluable lessons learned – the importance of resilience, the value of learning from failure, and the unwavering belief in the boundless possibilities that could be unlocked through the pursuit of entrepreneurial dreams, no matter the obstacles encountered along the way.

Chapter 25: Rebuilding Confidence

The journey of entrepreneurship is a rollercoaster of highs and lows, and Jennifer had experienced her fair share of both. As she emerged from the setback of her app's initial launch, she embarked on a transformative process of rebuilding her confidence and using her mistakes as stepping stones towards greater success.

The months following the relaunch of the app were marked by an unwavering commitment to continuous improvement. Jennifer and her team closely monitored user feedback, conducted regular updates, and prioritized user experience above all else. The iterative process was a testament to Jennifer's resilience and her determination to turn her setbacks into a springboard for growth.

Jennifer's relationship with failure had evolved. Rather than viewing it as a mark of defeat, she embraced it as a valuable teacher. Each challenge, each obstacle, and each mistake became an opportunity to learn, adapt, and refine her approach. Jennifer's willingness to confront her shortcomings head-on was a reflection of her courage and her unwavering belief in her own potential.

One of the most significant lessons Jennifer had learned was the importance of effective communication. As the app underwent transformations, Jennifer made a conscious effort to engage with users transparently. She communicated the changes, explained the rationale behind decisions, and actively sought user input. The open dialogue fostered a sense of community and trust, enabling Jennifer to rebuild the confidence of her user base.

But the journey of rebuilding confidence extended beyond the app itself. Jennifer found herself confronting her own inner doubts and insecurities. The setback had momentarily shaken her self-assurance, but Jennifer was determined to reclaim her sense of empowerment. She engaged in self-reflection, sought support from mentors, and practiced self-compassion.

Jennifer's mentor, Elizabeth, played a pivotal role in this process. With her guidance, Jennifer explored the concept of imposter syndrome – the tendency to doubt one's own accomplishments and feel undeserving of success. Elizabeth's words became a beacon of reassurance: "Jennifer, remember that setbacks are not a reflection of your worth. Embrace your journey, own your achievements, and continue to learn and grow."

As Jennifer continued to pour her energy into the app and her other ventures, she witnessed a gradual resurgence in user engagement and positive feedback. The turnaround was a testament to her resilience, her ability to learn from her mistakes, and her commitment to providing value to her users.

One day, as Jennifer scrolled through user testimonials and messages of gratitude, a sense of pride and accomplishment washed over her. The journey of rebuilding confidence had been arduous, but it had reinforced Jennifer's belief in her ability to overcome challenges and create impact.

The experience had transformed Jennifer's relationship with failure. She no longer feared it; instead, she embraced it as an integral part of the entrepreneurial process. Failure had become a stepping stone towards growth, a catalyst for innovation, and a reminder of the extraordinary capacity within her to persevere and thrive.

As Jennifer looked ahead to the horizon, she carried with her the lessons learned – the importance of resilience, the value of self-compassion, and the unwavering belief in the boundless possibilities that could be unlocked through the journey of entrepreneurship. Through the process of rebuilding confidence, Jennifer had not only strengthened her resolve as an entrepreneur but had also cultivated a deeper sense of empowerment that would continue to fuel her journey towards success.

Chapter 26: Innovative Idea

In the world of entrepreneurship, ideas are the lifeblood of innovation. They have the power to disrupt industries, solve pressing problems, and create transformative change. It was during a moment of contemplation and inspiration that Jennifer conceived a groundbreaking business concept that would push the boundaries of finance and technology.

Late one evening, as Jennifer gazed out of her window, her mind began to wander. She pondered the evolving landscape of finance, the challenges individuals faced in managing their financial lives, and the untapped potential of technology. The intersection of these thoughts gave rise to a revolutionary idea – a platform that harnessed artificial intelligence (AI) and machine learning to provide personalized, data-driven financial advice.

The concept was ambitious. Jennifer envisioned an AI-powered financial companion that would analyze users' financial habits, goals, and behaviors. The platform would leverage sophisticated algorithms to generate tailored recommendations, identify potential pitfalls, and guide users towards sound financial decisions. It was a vision rooted in the belief that technology could democratize access to financial expertise and empower individuals to make informed choices.

Jennifer's excitement was palpable as she began to flesh out the details of her innovative idea. She sketched out wireframes, outlined user interfaces, and mapped the architecture of the AI platform. The vision was grand, but Jennifer recognized that the path from concept to reality would be marked by challenges, technical complexities, and the need for interdisciplinary collaboration.

With unwavering determination, Jennifer embarked on a journey to bring her innovative idea to life. She assembled a multidisciplinary team of experts – from data scientists and engineers to user experience designers and financial analysts. The collaboration was characterized by a shared passion for innovation and a commitment to realizing the potential of AI in the world of finance.

The early stages of development were marked by intense research and experimentation. Jennifer's team delved into the intricacies of machine learning, data analytics, and natural language processing. They fine-tuned algorithms, refined predictive models, and created a data infrastructure that would enable the platform to learn and adapt over time.

The journey was not without its challenges. Technical hurdles, ethical considerations, and the need to ensure data privacy were constant companions. Jennifer and her team navigated uncharted waters, seeking guidance from experts, conducting rigorous testing, and iterating on their approach.

Months of dedicated effort culminated in the launch of "FinAI: Your Financial Companion." The platform represented the realization of Jennifer's visionary concept – an AI-powered tool that harnessed the power of data to provide users with actionable insights, personalized recommendations, and a comprehensive view of their financial health. The response from users was enthusiastic, with individuals expressing gratitude for the platform's ability to simplify complex financial decisions.

But Jennifer's journey didn't end with the platform's launch. She recognized that the evolution of "FinAI" was a continuous process, one that required ongoing innovation, user feedback, and adaptation. Jennifer's commitment to pushing the boundaries of technology and finance remained unwavering, and she continued to lead her team in refining and expanding the capabilities of the platform.

As Jennifer looked back on the path that had led her to conceive and execute her innovative idea, she marveled at the transformative power of entrepreneurship. The journey from inspiration to execution had been a testament to her resilience, her ability to collaborate across disciplines, and her belief in the boundless possibilities that could be unlocked through the pursuit of groundbreaking concepts.

And as Jennifer looked ahead to the horizon, she carried with her the lessons learned – the importance of bold ideas, the value of interdisciplinary collaboration, and the unwavering belief in the extraordinary capacity within her to innovate, create, and leave a lasting mark on the world of business and finance.

Chapter 27: Seeking Investors

With "FinAI: Your Financial Companion" up and running, Jennifer's innovative idea had taken a tangible form, offering users personalized financial guidance through the power of artificial intelligence. However, to propel her platform to new heights and drive widespread adoption, Jennifer knew that she needed the support of investors who shared her vision and believed in the transformative potential of her concept.

The journey of seeking investors was a new frontier for Jennifer, one that required a unique set of skills and strategies. Armed with a compelling pitch deck, a clear value proposition, and an unwavering passion for her platform, Jennifer embarked on a mission to secure the financial backing needed to fuel her ambitious goals.

Her first opportunity came at a local startup pitch event. Nervous yet determined, Jennifer took the stage to present "FinAI" to a room filled with potential investors, venture capitalists, and fellow entrepreneurs. She eloquently outlined the platform's features, demonstrated its AI-powered capabilities, and passionately conveyed her vision for revolutionizing the financial industry.

As Jennifer spoke, she felt a surge of confidence and conviction. Her passion was palpable, and her mastery of the subject matter resonated with the audience. Questions were posed, discussions ensued, and Jennifer found herself engaged in meaningful conversations about the future of AI-driven financial solutions.

The pitch event marked the beginning of Jennifer's journey to secure investors. She met with venture capital firms, angel investors, and individuals who specialized in fintech innovation. Each meeting presented an opportunity to share her story, showcase the platform's potential, and address questions and concerns.

However, Jennifer soon realized that the path to securing investment was not without its challenges. Some potential backers were intrigued by the concept but had reservations about the platform's scalability and market fit. Others were skeptical about the competitive landscape and the complexities of integrating AI into the financial industry.

The rejections and hesitations were a sobering reminder that the road to securing investors was paved with uncertainty. But Jennifer's determination remained unshaken. She viewed each setback as an opportunity to refine her pitch, gather feedback, and strengthen her understanding of the investor landscape.

In the midst of her efforts, Jennifer received an unexpected email from an investor named Rebecca Davis. Rebecca had attended the pitch event where Jennifer had presented "FinAI" and was captivated by the platform's potential. Intrigued by Jennifer's vision and her commitment to financial empowerment, Rebecca expressed interest in a meeting.

The meeting with Rebecca proved to be a turning point. They engaged in a candid and insightful conversation, with Rebecca probing Jennifer about her business model, growth strategies, and long-term vision. Jennifer's responses were marked by a blend of strategic thinking and genuine enthusiasm, leaving a positive impression on Rebecca.

Weeks later, Jennifer received the news she had been eagerly anticipating – Rebecca and her investment firm had decided to back "FinAI: Your Financial Companion." The investment provided the financial infusion needed to accelerate platform development, expand user outreach, and further refine the AI-powered algorithms.

The support from Rebecca and her firm was a validation of Jennifer's dedication and a testament to the potential of her innovative idea. As "FinAI" continued to evolve and capture the attention of users, Jennifer recognized that securing investors was not just about financial backing, but about finding partners who shared her vision, believed in her mission, and were committed to driving positive change in the world of finance.

And as Jennifer looked ahead to the future, she carried with her the lessons learned – the importance of resilience, the value of strategic networking, and the unwavering belief in the transformative potential of seeking investors who could help turn innovative ideas into reality. Through the process of pitching her platform to potential backers, Jennifer had not only secured the resources needed to propel "FinAI" forward but had also cultivated a deeper understanding of the intricate dance between entrepreneurship and investment.

Chapter 28: The Journey Begins

With the backing of investor Rebecca Davis and her firm, Jennifer's vision for "FinAI: Your Financial Companion" was poised to take flight. The infusion of funding provided the resources needed to accelerate platform development, enhance user experience, and expand outreach efforts. The journey from idea to execution had been marked by determination, innovation, and a deep commitment to driving positive change in the world of finance.

As Jennifer stood before her team, a sense of anticipation hung in the air. The months of hard work, collaboration, and refinement had led to this moment – the official launch of "FinAI." The platform had undergone significant transformations, with its AI-powered algorithms fine-tuned to provide users with even more personalized and insightful financial guidance.

The launch strategy was meticulously planned, with a focus on generating buzz, driving user engagement, and showcasing the platform's unique value proposition. Jennifer's team orchestrated a comprehensive marketing campaign that included social media teasers, influencer partnerships, and a series of informative webinars that highlighted the platform's capabilities.

The response was nothing short of extraordinary. On the day of the launch, "FinAI" garnered thousands of sign-ups within hours, a testament to the anticipation that had been building in the lead-up to the release. Users from diverse backgrounds, ranging from recent graduates to seasoned investors, expressed enthusiasm for the platform's potential to transform their financial lives.

Jennifer's journey had come full circle – from conceiving a groundbreaking idea to securing investment and launching her business. The path had been marked by challenges, setbacks, and moments of triumph. As she watched users engage with "FinAI,"

Jennifer felt a deep sense of fulfillment and a renewed commitment to her mission of democratizing access to financial expertise.

The platform's impact was visible in the stories of users who found clarity in their financial goals, made informed decisions, and gained confidence in managing their finances. Jennifer's inbox was flooded with messages of gratitude and testimonials that underscored the transformative power of "FinAI."

One particular message stood out – an email from a single mother who had struggled to make sense of her financial situation. With the guidance of "FinAI," she had developed a budget, optimized her savings, and even started investing for her daughter's future. The message ended with a heartfelt note of appreciation, thanking Jennifer for creating a platform that had made a tangible difference in her life.

As Jennifer read the email, tears welled up in her eyes. It was a reminder that her journey as an entrepreneur was not just about business growth and financial success. It was about creating meaningful impact, empowering individuals to make positive changes, and leaving a lasting legacy that resonated with the spirit of her mother's unwavering support and belief in her potential.

The launch of "FinAI: Your Financial Companion" marked a new chapter in Jennifer's journey – one characterized by innovation, impact, and the relentless pursuit of excellence. Jennifer's dedication to her mission had been unwavering, and as she looked ahead to the horizon, she carried with her the lessons learned – the importance of resilience, the value of collaboration, and the unwavering belief in the boundless possibilities that could be unlocked through the journey of entrepreneurship.

And so, the journey had begun – a journey that held the promise of growth, learning, and continued impact. As Jennifer continued to navigate the dynamic landscape of business and finance, she carried with her the spirit of her mother's love, the wisdom of her mentors, and the unyielding determination to make a difference, one innovative idea at a time.

Chapter 29: Navigating Entrepreneurship

As the excitement of the "FinAI" launch settled, Jennifer found herself immersed in the realities of running a thriving company. The journey of entrepreneurship had brought her triumphs, but it also demanded a deep understanding of the complexities, challenges, and responsibilities that came with building and scaling a business.

The initial surge of sign-ups and user engagement had been a testament to the platform's value, but it also presented Jennifer with the task of managing rapid growth. The influx of users highlighted the importance of robust infrastructure, reliable customer support, and seamless user experiences. Jennifer's team worked tirelessly to ensure that the platform's performance met the heightened demand.

Scaling the company also meant expanding the team. Jennifer faced the responsibility of recruiting, onboarding, and nurturing a group of talented individuals who shared her vision and could contribute to the platform's ongoing success. The role of a leader came with its own set of challenges – from fostering a culture of innovation to providing mentorship and guidance.

Amidst the operational demands, Jennifer encountered regulatory complexities that were inherent to the finance industry. Compliance, data privacy, and legal considerations became integral aspects of her responsibilities. Jennifer navigated through the intricate landscape, seeking expert advice and ensuring that "FinAI" remained compliant with industry standards.

Financial sustainability was another facet of entrepreneurship that Jennifer grappled with. While the backing of investors had provided the initial funding, the company's growth required ongoing financial planning, budget allocation, and a clear revenue strategy. Jennifer engaged with financial advisors and experts to chart a course towards long-term sustainability.

In the midst of these challenges, Jennifer's commitment to user-centricity remained steadfast. She continued to gather user feedback, conduct surveys, and analyze data to understand user needs and preferences. The insights gleaned from users guided iterative improvements, new feature development, and the evolution of the platform's AI algorithms.

As "FinAI" continued to flourish, Jennifer also recognized the importance of strategic partnerships. Collaborations with financial institutions, educational organizations, and other fintech players allowed her to expand the platform's reach, enhance its offerings, and tap into new opportunities for growth.

The journey of entrepreneurship had its moments of doubt and uncertainty. Jennifer faced sleepless nights, tough decisions, and moments of self-doubt. However, her ability to embrace challenges and persevere remained a testament to her resilience and determination.

Throughout the journey, Jennifer leaned on her mentors, her professional network, and her own experiences for guidance. She recalled the lessons learned from her mother's unwavering support, her mentor Elizabeth's wisdom, and her own transformational moments of triumph and setback.

One day, as Jennifer reviewed the progress of "FinAI" and reflected on the path she had traversed, she realized that the journey of entrepreneurship was a continuous evolution. It was about learning from mistakes, adapting to change, and maintaining a deep commitment to her vision. The realities of running a company had underscored the importance of adaptability, agility, and a growth mindset.

As Jennifer looked ahead to the horizon, she carried with her the lessons learned – the importance of resilience, the value of embracing challenges, and the unwavering belief in the boundless possibilities that could be unlocked through the journey of entrepreneurship. Her commitment to navigating the complexities of running a company was a testament to her dedication to making a lasting impact in the world of business and finance.

Chapter 30: Balancing Act

With "FinAI: Your Financial Companion" gaining traction and her company flourishing, Jennifer found herself in the midst of a demanding and exhilarating balancing act. The responsibilities of entrepreneurship were substantial, but Jennifer was determined to also uphold her commitment to her education, personal life, and overall well-being.

As she embarked on her business and finance degree at the university, Jennifer's schedule became a complex tapestry of classes, meetings, and study sessions. The rigors of academia demanded focus and diligence, and Jennifer applied the same determination and work ethic that had fueled her entrepreneurial journey. Balancing her coursework with the demands of running a company required careful time management and a strategic approach to prioritization.

Jennifer's days were marked by a seamless transition between the world of academia and the realm of entrepreneurship. She would attend lectures, actively participate in discussions, and engage with her professors and peers. In the moments between classes, she would immerse herself in the intricacies of "FinAI," collaborating with her team, strategizing marketing initiatives, and making crucial decisions to drive the platform's growth.

The evenings were often dedicated to furthering her studies, poring over textbooks, and completing assignments. Jennifer's ability to synthesize her academic learnings with her real-world experiences was a testament to her intellectual acumen and her dedication to both domains of her life.

But the balancing act extended beyond the realms of work and studies. Jennifer recognized the importance of nurturing her personal well-being and maintaining meaningful connections with family and friends. She carved out time for moments of relaxation, self-care, and leisure activities that rejuvenated her spirit and provided a respite from her demanding schedule.

Throughout her journey, Jennifer's support system played a pivotal role. Her aunt and uncle, who had taken her in after her mother's tragic passing, provided a stable and nurturing environment that allowed her to thrive. Her mentors, including Elizabeth and Rebecca, offered guidance, encouragement, and a sounding board for her ideas and challenges.

One of the most important lessons Jennifer had learned was the value of delegation and collaboration. She assembled a capable and dedicated team that shared her passion and commitment to the platform's mission. Delegating responsibilities allowed Jennifer to focus on strategic decisions, long-term planning, and fostering innovation, while also providing her team with opportunities to contribute and grow.

The balancing act also required a strong sense of self-awareness and the ability to recognize the signs of burnout or overwhelm. Jennifer was attuned to her own energy levels and stress triggers, and she embraced practices such as meditation, exercise, and journaling to maintain her mental and emotional well-being.

Despite the demands of her dual roles as a student and an entrepreneur, Jennifer found moments of joy and fulfillment in both realms. The sense of accomplishment she felt as she navigated her studies and guided her company through growth was a testament to her resilience, determination, and unwavering belief in her ability to succeed.

As Jennifer looked ahead to the future, she carried with her the lessons learned – the importance of balance, the value of self-care, and the unwavering belief in the boundless possibilities that could be unlocked through the art of juggling responsibilities. Her ability to seamlessly navigate the complex tapestry of work, studies, and personal life was a reflection of her commitment to holistic success and her unyielding determination to make a meaningful impact in every facet of her life.

Chapter 31: Love and Relationships

Amidst the dynamic landscape of entrepreneurship, academia, and personal growth, Jennifer's journey took an unexpected turn as she explored the realm of love and relationships. The demands of her busy life had often kept her focused on her studies and her business, but as she found herself connecting with like-minded individuals, she began to open her heart to the possibility of romance.

Jennifer's introduction to the world of romance came through a chance encounter at a networking event. As she engaged in a spirited conversation about fintech innovation, she found herself captivated by the insights and passion of a fellow attendee named Alex. Their discussions flowed seamlessly, and Jennifer felt a connection that extended beyond professional interests.

The friendship with Alex evolved over time, and they found themselves spending more moments together outside of work-related events. Shared interests, mutual respect, and a sense of ease marked their interactions. As their connection deepened, Jennifer felt a range of emotions – excitement, curiosity, and a hint of vulnerability as she navigated the unfamiliar terrain of romantic feelings.

Jennifer's journey into romance was a delicate balance, one that required her to navigate her newfound emotions while maintaining her commitments to her studies and her company. She found herself carving out moments of time for dates, conversations, and shared experiences with Alex, all while ensuring that her entrepreneurial pursuits remained a priority.

Through her relationship with Alex, Jennifer experienced moments of joy, companionship, and shared growth. The partnership was marked by a mutual understanding of each other's ambitions, challenges, and dreams. They supported one another's journeys, celebrated milestones, and provided a source of comfort amidst the highs and lows of their individual pursuits.

However, Jennifer's foray into romance also prompted moments of introspection. She grappled with questions about balancing personal and professional aspirations, communicating her boundaries, and nurturing her own well-being amidst the demands of her busy life. Jennifer's ability to communicate openly and honestly with Alex became a testament to her commitment to building a relationship that was rooted in trust and mutual understanding.

As Jennifer navigated the complexities of love and relationships, she drew upon the lessons learned from her entrepreneurial journey. Just as she had embraced challenges, sought guidance from mentors, and demonstrated resilience in the face of setbacks, Jennifer applied those same principles to her romantic journey. She recognized that love, like entrepreneurship, required intention, effort, and a willingness to evolve and adapt.

One day, as Jennifer and Alex strolled through a park, hand in hand, Jennifer felt a sense of contentment and gratitude. The journey of exploring romantic interests had brought her moments of joy, growth, and companionship. Just as her journey as an entrepreneur had shaped her into a resilient and empowered individual, her journey through love had enriched her life in unexpected ways.

As Jennifer looked ahead to the future, she carried with her the lessons learned – the importance of balance, the value of open communication, and the unwavering belief in the boundless possibilities that could be unlocked through the pursuit of love and relationships. Her ability to navigate the intricate dance between entrepreneurship and matters of the heart was a testament to her capacity for growth, her dedication to holistic well-being, and her unyielding determination to create a life that was both professionally and personally fulfilling.

Chapter 32: Empowering Others

Jennifer's journey of entrepreneurship had been marked by triumphs, challenges, and transformative growth. As her platform "FinAI: Your Financial Companion" continued to flourish, Jennifer recognized the importance of paying forward the knowledge, experiences, and insights she had gained along the way. This realization led her to embark on a new chapter – that of mentoring and empowering aspiring entrepreneurs.

Jennifer's commitment to mentoring was rooted in her belief that everyone should have the opportunity to pursue their dreams and create positive change in the world. She had experienced the profound impact of guidance and mentorship firsthand, from her mother's unwavering support to the advice of mentors like Elizabeth and Rebecca.

With a sense of purpose and a desire to make a difference, Jennifer began to actively engage with aspiring entrepreneurs, offering guidance, support, and a listening ear. She participated in startup incubators, spoke at entrepreneurship events, and even organized workshops that focused on various aspects of building and scaling a business.

One of Jennifer's mentees was Sarah, a young entrepreneur who had a vision for a sustainable fashion startup. Sarah's passion and drive resonated with Jennifer, and they quickly formed a mentor-mentee bond that would shape both of their journeys. Jennifer shared insights from her own experiences, offered strategic advice, and provided a source of encouragement as Sarah navigated the challenges of launching her own venture.

Through her interactions with mentees like Sarah, Jennifer realized the profound impact of mentorship on the entrepreneurial journey. She witnessed the transformative power of guidance and the role it played in accelerating growth, building confidence, and instilling a sense of resilience in aspiring entrepreneurs.

Jennifer's approach to mentoring was holistic. She encouraged her mentees to not only focus on business strategies but also to prioritize their well-being, personal growth, and work-life balance. Her own journey had taught her the importance of cultivating a mindset of resilience, adaptability, and self-care – principles she shared with her mentees.

As Jennifer's mentoring efforts continued to grow, she found herself reflecting on the interconnectedness of her roles as an entrepreneur, a student, and a mentor. The lessons she had learned, the challenges she had overcome, and the triumphs she had achieved all became valuable tools that she could use to empower and uplift others.

One day, as Jennifer spoke at an entrepreneurship event, she looked out at the eager faces of aspiring entrepreneurs in the audience. The energy and enthusiasm in the room were palpable, and Jennifer felt a deep sense of fulfillment. She recognized that her journey was no longer just about her own success – it was about creating a ripple effect of positive change, one mentorship at a time.

As Jennifer looked ahead to the future, she carried with her the lessons learned – the importance of giving back, the value of mentorship, and the unwavering belief in the boundless possibilities that could be unlocked through the act of empowering others. Her commitment to mentoring was a testament to her dedication to creating a legacy that extended far beyond her own achievements, one that inspired and uplifted the next generation of entrepreneurs to pursue their dreams, overcome challenges, and make a lasting impact in the world

Chapter 33: Expanding Horizons

The journey of entrepreneurship had been a remarkable one for Jennifer, filled with challenges, triumphs, and countless moments of growth. As "FinAI: Your Financial Companion" continued to gain traction and recognition, Jennifer found herself on the cusp of a new phase – one that would expand her horizons and propel her business to even greater heights.

The success of "FinAI" had attracted the attention of both users and industry experts alike. Positive reviews, word-of-mouth referrals, and media coverage had contributed to a steady influx of new users who were drawn to the platform's innovative approach to financial guidance. Jennifer's commitment to user-centricity had solidified "FinAI's" position as a trusted resource for individuals seeking to make informed financial decisions.

With a growing user base, Jennifer's business had evolved from a startup into a reputable player in the fintech industry. The recognition and accolades began to pour in, from industry awards to invitations to speak at conferences and events. Jennifer's unique journey – from a young girl who witnessed a tragic event to a successful entrepreneur – resonated with audiences and served as an inspiration to others.

One of the pivotal moments came when Jennifer was invited to deliver a keynote address at a prestigious international fintech conference. The opportunity was both an honor and a testament to the impact she had made in the industry. Standing on the stage, Jennifer shared her journey, her insights, and her vision for the future of finance.

Her words resonated with the audience, and the response was overwhelming. Attendees were captivated by Jennifer's story of resilience, innovation, and the pursuit of positive change. The keynote address marked a turning point, opening doors to new partnerships, collaborations, and opportunities that would further elevate the profile of "FinAI" and its mission.

Expanding horizons also meant venturing into new markets and exploring partnerships that aligned with Jennifer's vision. Collaborations with financial institutions, educational organizations, and community outreach initiatives allowed "FinAI" to reach diverse audiences and extend its impact beyond its original scope.

As the business grew, Jennifer remained committed to her role as a mentor and advocate for aspiring entrepreneurs. Her experiences and insights had become valuable tools that she could use to inspire others, guide their journeys, and foster a sense of empowerment within the entrepreneurial community.

Amidst the whirlwind of recognition and expansion, Jennifer remained grounded in her core values. The commitment to user empowerment, data privacy, and ethical fintech practices remained at the forefront of her decision-making. Every step forward was guided by a sense of purpose and a belief in the transformative potential of innovation.

As Jennifer looked ahead to the future, she carried with her the lessons learned – the importance of staying true to one's values, the value of mentorship and community, and the unwavering belief in the boundless possibilities that could be unlocked through the pursuit of excellence and positive impact. The journey of expanding horizons was a testament to her dedication to creating meaningful change in the world of business and finance, and her ability to navigate the complexities of growth with grace, authenticity, and an unwavering commitment to her vision.

Chapter 34: International Opportunities

The success and recognition of "FinAI: Your Financial Companion" had transcended borders, capturing the attention of individuals and organizations around the world. As Jennifer's platform gained traction, she found herself on the brink of exploring international opportunities that would take her entrepreneurial journey to new and exciting heights.

The idea of expanding into global markets was both exhilarating and challenging. Jennifer recognized that each market had its unique dynamics, cultural nuances, and regulatory landscapes. The prospect of introducing "FinAI" to diverse audiences ignited a sense of curiosity and possibility, driving Jennifer to embark on a journey of exploration and strategic planning.

To begin the process, Jennifer assembled a dedicated team with expertise in international business, market research, and cross-cultural communication. Together, they conducted in-depth analyses of potential target markets, assessing factors such as user demographics, financial behaviors, and competitive landscapes.

The research revealed a world of opportunities – from emerging economies with a growing middle class to established financial hubs seeking innovative solutions. Jennifer's platform had the potential to address the diverse financial needs of individuals across the globe, providing personalized guidance and insights that transcended cultural boundaries.

One of the markets that piqued Jennifer's interest was India, a country characterized by a rapidly expanding fintech ecosystem and a burgeoning interest in digital financial solutions. Jennifer recognized the potential to make a meaningful impact in a market where financial literacy and empowerment were paramount.

Jennifer's journey into international expansion was marked by strategic partnerships and collaborative efforts. She engaged with local experts, formed alliances with fintech associations, and leveraged insights from her mentorship network to navigate the complexities of entering a new market.

The process of adapting "FinAI" for the Indian market required careful consideration. Jennifer's team worked diligently to ensure that the platform's AI algorithms were optimized to address the unique financial behaviors and goals of Indian users. The user interface was adapted to resonate with cultural preferences, and localization efforts ensured that the platform's content and messaging were relevant and relatable.

The launch of "FinAI" in India was met with enthusiasm and positive reception. Users embraced the platform's personalized financial guidance, viewing it as a valuable tool to navigate the complexities of their financial lives. The success in India marked the beginning of a broader international expansion strategy, with Jennifer's platform making its way to other countries, each with its own set of opportunities and challenges.

As Jennifer's platform continued to expand its global footprint, she found herself reflecting on the interconnectedness of the world and the transformative power of technology to bridge gaps, facilitate communication, and drive positive change on a global scale. The journey of exploring international markets was not just about business growth – it was about creating a ripple effect of empowerment, education, and financial well-being that transcended borders and touched the lives of individuals from diverse backgrounds.

As Jennifer looked ahead to the future, she carried with her the lessons learned – the importance of adaptability, the value of cross-cultural collaboration, and the unwavering belief in the boundless possibilities that could be unlocked through the pursuit of international opportunities. Her commitment to exploring global markets was a testament to her dedication to making a meaningful impact in the world of business and finance, one market at a time.

Chapter 35: Scaling Up

The journey of entrepreneurship had been a transformative one for Jennifer, marked by resilience, innovation, and a relentless pursuit of positive change. As "FinAI: Your Financial Companion" continued to gain momentum and explore international markets, Jennifer found herself navigating a new phase – the exhilarating challenge of scaling up her company.

The rapid growth of "FinAI" presented Jennifer with a unique set of opportunities and complexities. The user base had expanded exponentially, and the platform's impact was being felt by individuals around the world. The demand for personalized financial guidance was evident, and Jennifer was determined to ensure that "FinAI" could reach even more users while maintaining the high standard of excellence that had become its hallmark.

Scaling up required a multifaceted approach. Jennifer's team expanded to include experts in technology, data science, customer support, and international operations. The organizational structure evolved to accommodate the growing demands, with Jennifer overseeing strategic decisions, partnerships, and the overarching vision.

One of the key challenges Jennifer faced was optimizing the platform's infrastructure to handle the increased load. The technological backbone of "FinAI" needed to be robust, scalable, and capable of providing seamless user experiences even as user numbers continued to surge. Jennifer worked closely with her technology team to ensure that the platform's performance met the heightened demand.

As the company scaled, Jennifer's role also evolved. She found herself delegating responsibilities, empowering her team members, and fostering a culture of innovation and collaboration. Jennifer's ability to inspire and lead became essential as she guided her team through the complexities of growth and transformation.

Strategic partnerships played a crucial role in the company's scaling efforts. Collaborations with financial institutions, educational organizations, and international partners allowed "FinAI" to tap into new markets, access valuable resources, and drive further growth. These partnerships were a testament to the platform's impact and its potential to revolutionize the way individuals approached their finances.

Amidst the whirlwind of scaling, Jennifer remained committed to her values of user empowerment, ethical fintech practices, and positive impact. She continued to gather user feedback, iterate on the platform's features, and ensure that "FinAI" remained a trusted resource that aligned with the diverse needs of its global user base.

The journey of scaling up was a learning experience for Jennifer – one that required her to embrace change, adapt to new dynamics, and remain agile in the face of evolving challenges. It was a testament to her ability to combine strategic thinking with a deep commitment to user-centricity, fostering a sense of community, and creating lasting value.

As Jennifer looked ahead to the future, she carried with her the lessons learned – the importance of adaptability, the value of strategic partnerships, and the unwavering belief in the boundless possibilities that could be unlocked through the pursuit of scaling up. Her commitment to expanding the reach and impact of "FinAI" was a testament to her dedication to creating meaningful change in the world of business and finance, and her ability to navigate the complexities of growth with grace, determination, and an unwavering commitment to her vision.

Chapter 36: Dealing with Competition

Jennifer's journey of entrepreneurship had been a remarkable one, characterized by innovation, growth, and a commitment to empowering individuals through "FinAI: Your Financial Companion." As her platform continued to flourish, Jennifer found herself facing a new and formidable challenge – competition from rival businesses that sought to make their mark in the fintech landscape.

The emergence of competitors was a testament to the impact that "FinAI" had made in the industry. Jennifer's platform had disrupted traditional approaches to financial guidance and had set a new standard for user-centric fintech solutions. The success of "FinAI" had captured the attention of other entrepreneurs and businesses eager to carve out their own space in the market.

The realization that her platform was no longer operating in isolation brought a mix of emotions for Jennifer – from a sense of validation to a heightened awareness of the need to innovate and stay ahead. Jennifer recognized that competition was a natural part of the entrepreneurial landscape, a driving force that pushed her to continuously evolve, adapt, and redefine her approach.

Jennifer's response to competition was rooted in her commitment to her users and her dedication to delivering value. She viewed competition as an opportunity to further hone "FinAI's" offerings, enhance user experiences, and elevate the platform's impact. Rather than shying away from the challenge, Jennifer embraced it as a catalyst for growth and innovation.

To address the competition, Jennifer's approach was multifaceted. She leveraged her team's expertise in data science and AI to refine the platform's algorithms, ensuring that "FinAI" provided even more accurate and personalized financial guidance. New features were developed based on user feedback and emerging trends, solidifying "FinAI's" position as a forward-thinking and user-focused solution.

Jennifer also recognized the importance of differentiation and brand identity. She collaborated with her marketing team to craft compelling narratives that highlighted "FinAI's" unique value proposition, its mission of empowerment, and its track record of positive impact. Jennifer's ability to articulate the platform's story set "FinAI" apart and resonated with users who sought more than just a financial tool – they sought a partner on their journey to financial well-being.

In the face of competition, Jennifer remained steadfast in her commitment to ethical fintech practices and user privacy. She emphasized transparency, data security, and user control as core tenets of "FinAI's" approach. Jennifer's unwavering dedication to user trust and empowerment fortified her platform's position in a competitive landscape.

Through the challenges posed by competition, Jennifer also found a renewed sense of purpose and determination. She drew upon the lessons she had learned throughout her entrepreneurial journey – the importance of resilience, the value of collaboration, and the unwavering belief in the boundless possibilities that could be unlocked through the pursuit of excellence.

As Jennifer looked ahead to the future, she carried with her the lessons learned – the importance of embracing competition, the value of differentiation, and the unwavering belief in the boundless possibilities that could be unlocked through the pursuit of innovation. Her ability to navigate the complexities of competition was a testament to her resilience, her strategic acumen, and her unyielding commitment to creating meaningful change in the world of business and finance.

Chapter 37: Ethical Dilemmas

Jennifer's journey of entrepreneurship had been marked by triumphs, challenges, and moments of transformation. As "FinAI: Your Financial Companion" continued to grow and evolve, Jennifer found herself facing a series of ethical dilemmas that tested her values, principles, and commitment to responsible business practices.

The success of "FinAI" had not only attracted users and recognition but had also garnered attention from potential investors and partners. Jennifer's platform had become a valuable asset in the eyes of those who saw the potential for financial gain. Offers for strategic alliances and partnerships poured in, each promising growth and expansion.

However, amidst the allure of these opportunities, Jennifer found herself confronted with ethical considerations that demanded careful thought and introspection. The decisions she made could shape the trajectory of her business and its impact on users, stakeholders, and the broader fintech ecosystem.

One such dilemma arose when a large financial institution expressed interest in acquiring "FinAI." The offer was substantial, promising financial security and resources that could accelerate the platform's growth. Yet, Jennifer grappled with questions about maintaining the platform's independence, user-centric focus, and commitment to ethical practices.

Jennifer convened her team and engaged in candid discussions about the potential acquisition. They weighed the pros and cons, considering the implications for user data privacy, platform autonomy, and the alignment of values. Jennifer's ability to foster an open and transparent dialogue within her team was a testament to her leadership and her commitment to making decisions that were grounded in ethical considerations.

Ultimately, Jennifer decided to decline the acquisition offer, choosing to preserve "FinAI's" integrity and independence. The decision was not without challenges, as it meant forgoing immediate financial gains. However, Jennifer remained resolute in her belief that staying true to her values and the platform's mission was paramount.

Another ethical dilemma arose when an advertising agency proposed a partnership that would involve using user data to target personalized financial advertisements. While the partnership had the potential to generate significant revenue, Jennifer grappled with concerns about user consent, data privacy, and the potential exploitation of vulnerable individuals.

Jennifer's response to the ethical dilemma was clear and unwavering. She declined the partnership, choosing to prioritize user trust, data privacy, and the platform's commitment to ethical use of user information. The decision was a reflection of Jennifer's dedication to putting the well-being of her users above short-term financial gains.

As Jennifer navigated these ethical dilemmas, she found herself drawing upon the lessons she had learned throughout her journey – the importance of staying true to her values, the value of open communication, and the unwavering belief in the boundless possibilities that could be unlocked through the pursuit of ethical business practices.

The ethical dilemmas Jennifer faced were not without challenges and sacrifices, but they reinforced her position as a principled and responsible entrepreneur. Her ability to make tough decisions that were guided by integrity and a commitment to doing what was right set a powerful example for her team, her peers, and the broader business community.

As Jennifer looked ahead to the future, she carried with her the lessons learned – the importance of ethical considerations, the value of staying true to one's values, and the unwavering belief in the boundless possibilities that could be unlocked through the pursuit of responsible and ethical entrepreneurship. Her ability to navigate the complexities of ethical dilemmas was a testament to her character, her leadership, and her unyielding commitment to creating a positive and lasting impact in the world of business and finance.

Chapter 38: Ethical Crossroads

Jennifer's journey as an entrepreneur had been a dynamic one, marked by innovation, growth, and a resolute commitment to ethical business practices. As "FinAI: Your Financial Companion" continued to thrive, Jennifer found herself navigating a series of profound ethical dilemmas that would test her principles and shape the course of her business.

One of the ethical crossroads Jennifer encountered involved a potential partnership with a financial institution known for predatory lending practices. The institution offered a substantial financial incentive in exchange for integrating their services into the "FinAI" platform. While the financial infusion could fuel growth, Jennifer was faced with a moral dilemma – should she compromise the platform's integrity for short-term gains?

Jennifer's decision-making process was meticulous and thoughtful. She convened her team to deliberate the potential partnership, engaging in candid discussions about the implications of associating with an institution that conflicted with "FinAI's" mission of empowering users with responsible financial guidance. The team's collaborative approach and commitment to ethical considerations echoed Jennifer's core values.

Ultimately, Jennifer chose to decline the partnership. Her decision was rooted in a deep commitment to user well-being, ethical financial practices, and the platform's unwavering dedication to promoting financial literacy and empowerment. The choice demonstrated Jennifer's courage to prioritize long-term impact over immediate financial incentives, setting a precedent for ethical decision-making within her company.

Another ethical dilemma arose when "FinAI" was presented with an opportunity to monetize user data by selling it to third-party advertisers. The financial gains from such a venture were tempting, but

Jennifer recognized the potential intrusion into user privacy and the ethical responsibility to safeguard user information.

Jennifer's response to this dilemma was resolute. She chose to protect user privacy and data integrity, rejecting the proposition to monetize user data. Instead, she explored alternative revenue streams that aligned with "FinAI's" values and principles, showcasing her commitment to putting user interests ahead of short-term profits.

Navigating these ethical dilemmas tested Jennifer's resolve and underscored her role as a principled leader. Her ability to make tough decisions that aligned with her moral compass set a powerful example for her team, stakeholders, and the broader entrepreneurial community. Jennifer's unwavering commitment to ethics was not just a business strategy – it was a reflection of her character and a testament to the positive change she aimed to create.

As Jennifer looked to the future, she carried with her the lessons learned – the importance of ethical considerations, the value of upholding principles, and the unwavering belief in the boundless possibilities that could be unlocked through the pursuit of responsible and morally upright entrepreneurship. Her ability to navigate the complexities of ethical dilemmas was a testament to her integrity, her leadership, and her unyielding dedication to creating a business that not only achieved success but also made a meaningful and ethical impact in the world.

Chapter 39: Making a Difference

Jennifer's entrepreneurial journey had been defined by innovation, growth, and a commitment to creating positive change through "FinAI: Your Financial Companion." As her platform continued to evolve, Jennifer recognized the profound opportunity to incorporate social responsibility into the fabric of her company, igniting a new chapter focused on making a difference beyond financial empowerment.

The realization that "FinAI" could serve as a catalyst for social impact led Jennifer to embark on a mission to integrate social responsibility into her business model. She envisioned a future where "FinAI" not only provided personalized financial guidance but also played a role in addressing broader societal challenges.

One of Jennifer's first steps was to establish a formal corporate social responsibility (CSR) program within her company. The program's pillars centered on financial education, community engagement, and sustainable practices. Jennifer's commitment to social responsibility permeated every aspect of the business, from strategic decision-making to day-to-day operations.

The financial education component of the CSR program involved partnering with educational institutions, community organizations, and non-profits to deliver financial literacy workshops and resources to underserved communities. Jennifer recognized that equipping individuals with essential financial skills could empower them to make informed decisions, break cycles of poverty, and build a brighter future.

Community engagement initiatives became a cornerstone of "FinAI's" social responsibility efforts. Jennifer's team organized volunteer activities, fundraisers, and partnerships with local organizations that aligned with causes such as education, healthcare, and environmental sustainability. Jennifer's ability to mobilize her team and inspire a sense of purpose demonstrated her leadership in fostering positive change.

Incorporating sustainable practices was another dimension of "FinAI's" social responsibility journey. Jennifer championed initiatives to reduce the company's environmental footprint, from minimizing waste to adopting renewable energy sources. By prioritizing sustainability, Jennifer aimed to create a business model that aligned with the long-term well-being of both users and the planet.

One of the defining moments of "FinAI's" social responsibility journey came when Jennifer launched the "Empower for Good" initiative. Through this program, a percentage of "FinAI's" profits were dedicated to funding social impact projects, scholarships, and grants that supported initiatives aligned with the platform's values. The initiative galvanized users, partners, and stakeholders, demonstrating the power of collective action for positive change.

As "FinAI" integrated social responsibility into its core, Jennifer's vision began to materialize. The platform's impact extended beyond individual financial empowerment to become a force for societal transformation. Jennifer's ability to leverage her business as a tool for meaningful change showcased her dedication to creating a legacy of positive impact.

Looking ahead, Jennifer carried with her the lessons learned – the importance of social responsibility, the value of community engagement, and the unwavering belief in the boundless possibilities that could be unlocked through the pursuit of making a difference. Her commitment to social impact was a testament to her values, her leadership, and her unyielding determination to create a business that not only achieved financial success but also left a lasting legacy of positive change in the world.

Chapter 40: Personal Growth

Jennifer's journey as an entrepreneur had been a remarkable one, filled with triumphs, challenges, and transformative moments. As she looked back on the path she had traveled with "FinAI: Your Financial Companion," Jennifer found herself immersed in a period of deep reflection, contemplating the profound personal growth she had experienced throughout her entrepreneurial journey.

The evolution from a young girl who witnessed a tragic event to a successful entrepreneur had been a testament to Jennifer's resilience, determination, and unwavering belief in the power of positive change. Her journey had not only shaped her business but had also shaped her as an individual, instilling in her a sense of purpose, a commitment to values, and a profound understanding of her own potential.

In the quiet moments of reflection, Jennifer recognized the pivotal role her mother had played in her life's trajectory. Her mother's love, acceptance, and unwavering support had laid the foundation for Jennifer's resilience and determination. The memory of her mother's dreams and aspirations continued to inspire Jennifer, serving as a constant reminder of the importance of pursuing one's passions with unwavering dedication.

The challenges and setbacks Jennifer had encountered along the way had become sources of strength and wisdom. Each obstacle had presented an opportunity for growth, resilience, and learning. Jennifer's ability to persevere in the face of adversity had fortified her character and empowered her to overcome even the most daunting of challenges.

Jennifer's personal growth had also been deeply intertwined with her role as a mentor and advocate for aspiring entrepreneurs. The act of empowering others and sharing her insights had not only enriched the lives of her mentees but had also deepened Jennifer's own understanding of leadership, empathy, and the profound impact of paying forward one's experiences.

As Jennifer reflected on her journey, she marveled at the interconnectedness of her experiences – from facing personal tragedy to transforming that pain into a driving force for positive change. Her ability to channel adversity into innovation, resilience, and compassion had become a testament to the extraordinary potential within every individual to create meaningful and lasting impact.

Looking ahead to the future, Jennifer carried with her the lessons learned – the importance of personal growth, the value of resilience, and the unwavering belief in the boundless possibilities that could be unlocked through the pursuit of one's dreams. Her journey of personal growth was a testament to her capacity for transformation, her dedication to creating positive change, and her unyielding determination to leave a legacy that inspired others to embrace their own journeys of growth and empowerment.

Chapter 41: Legacy of Strength

Jennifer's entrepreneurial journey had been defined by resilience, innovation, and an unwavering commitment to creating positive change through "FinAI: Your Financial Companion." As she stood on the precipice of new horizons, Jennifer found herself drawn to a profound mission – to honor her mother's memory and create a lasting legacy of strength, love, and empowerment.

The memory of Jennifer's mother, Emily, had been a guiding light throughout her journey. Emily's unwavering support, love, and acceptance had shaped Jennifer's character, instilling in her the values of compassion, determination, and the belief in the power of dreams. As Jennifer's platform continued to evolve and flourish, she saw an opportunity to weave her mother's legacy into the very fabric of her business.

With a heart full of purpose, Jennifer embarked on a series of initiatives that celebrated and honored her mother's memory. One of the first steps was the establishment of the "Emily Legacy Foundation." Through this foundation, Jennifer aimed to empower underprivileged individuals by providing access to financial education, resources, and opportunities for personal and professional growth. The foundation became a living testament to the love and resilience that had defined her mother's spirit.

In collaboration with the foundation, Jennifer launched the "Dreams Ignited" scholarship program. This initiative provided scholarships to aspiring entrepreneurs, particularly those who had faced adversity or challenges in their lives. The program aimed to ignite the spark of ambition and create a ripple effect of positive change, just as Jennifer's mother had done for her.

Another integral part of Jennifer's tribute to her mother was the annual "Emily Awards." These awards celebrated individuals and organizations that exemplified the qualities of empathy, determination, and a commitment to social impact. The awards not only recognized outstanding contributions but also served as a platform to inspire and uplift others on their own journeys of making a difference.

Jennifer's platform, "FinAI," played a pivotal role in bringing her mother's legacy to life. A dedicated section of the platform was devoted to sharing Emily's story – a tale of strength, love, and unwavering support. Users could draw inspiration from Emily's journey, connecting with the values that underpinned "FinAI's" mission of empowerment and responsible financial guidance.

The legacy of strength that Jennifer cultivated became a driving force, infusing her business with purpose and inspiring others to embrace their own potential. The "Emily Legacy Foundation" touched countless lives, offering hope, opportunity, and the tools needed to overcome adversity and achieve dreams.

As Jennifer looked ahead to the future, she carried with her the lessons learned – the importance of honoring loved ones, the value of creating a legacy of positive impact, and the unwavering belief in the boundless possibilities that could be unlocked through the pursuit of meaningful change. Her tribute to her mother's memory was a testament to her resilience, her compassion, and her unyielding dedication to leaving a lasting legacy of strength and empowerment in the world.

Chapter 42: Facing the Past

Jennifer's journey had been one of resilience, growth, and unwavering determination. As "FinAI: Your Financial Companion" continued to thrive, Jennifer found herself facing a deeply personal and emotionally charged chapter – the confrontation with her mother's murderer, a pivotal step towards closure and healing.

The memories of that tragic night had haunted Jennifer's thoughts for years, a constant reminder of the pain and loss she had endured. The decision to confront her mother's murderer was not made lightly, but Jennifer recognized that facing the past was an essential part of her journey towards healing and finding a sense of closure.

Gathering her courage, Jennifer embarked on a journey to seek out the truth and confront the person responsible for her mother's death. With the support of a dedicated team of investigators, she delved into the details of the case, meticulously piecing together evidence and unearthing long-buried secrets.

The process was emotionally taxing, as Jennifer revisited painful memories and grappled with the weight of her loss. Yet, her determination remained unwavering, driven by the need to find answers and hold the perpetrator accountable for their actions.

As the pieces of the puzzle fell into place, Jennifer found herself face to face with the person who had shattered her world. The confrontation was a mix of emotions – anger, grief, and a profound desire for justice. Jennifer's ability to confront her mother's murderer demonstrated her incredible strength and resilience, as she channeled her pain into a pursuit of truth and closure.

During the confrontation, Jennifer sought not only answers but also a sense of understanding. She engaged in a dialogue that delved into the motivations behind the tragic event, the impact it had on her life, and the ripple effects it had on both their lives. The conversation was raw, emotional, and a cathartic step towards coming to terms with the past.

The confrontation marked a turning point in Jennifer's journey of healing. It was not about seeking revenge, but rather about reclaiming her agency, finding closure, and taking control of her narrative. Jennifer's ability to confront the past head-on was a testament to her resilience, her capacity for forgiveness, and her unwavering commitment to finding strength in the face of adversity.

As Jennifer looked ahead to the future, she carried with her the lessons learned – the importance of confronting the past, the value of seeking closure, and the unwavering belief in the boundless possibilities that could be unlocked through the pursuit of healing and growth. Her ability to face the past was a testament to her courage, her resilience, and her unyielding determination to find peace and move forward with a renewed sense of purpose and strength.

Chapter 43: Healing Wounds

Jennifer's journey had been one of transformation, growth, and resilience. As "FinAI: Your Financial Companion" continued to make an impact, Jennifer found herself on a path of profound healing, one that led her towards closure, forgiveness, and a newfound sense of peace.

The journey to healing had been arduous, marked by confronting painful memories, seeking answers, and facing her mother's murderer. Yet, as Jennifer navigated the complexities of her emotions, she discovered that the power of healing lay not in revenge or bitterness, but in the capacity to forgive.

Forgiveness was not a simple decision but a process, one that required Jennifer to delve deep within herself and confront her own pain and anger. It was a journey of self-discovery, a path towards releasing the heavy burden that had weighed on her heart for so long.

As Jennifer worked through her emotions, she found solace in a support network that included friends, mentors, and a counselor who had been a guiding light throughout her journey. Together, they helped Jennifer navigate the emotional terrain, providing a safe space for her to express her feelings, reflect on her experiences, and find a path towards forgiveness.

The turning point came during a moment of quiet reflection. Jennifer sat amidst nature, the gentle rustling of leaves and the soothing sound of a flowing stream creating a backdrop of serenity. In that stillness, Jennifer made a conscious decision – a decision to let go of the anger, resentment, and pain that had held her captive for so long.

Forgiveness, Jennifer realized, was not about absolving the perpetrator or condoning the crime. It was about freeing herself from the shackles of hatred and allowing herself to heal. Through forgiveness, Jennifer found the strength to rise above the darkness that had consumed her, embracing a newfound sense of lightness and liberation.

The act of forgiveness was not just a gift to the person who had caused her pain; it was a profound gift to herself. It was a way for Jennifer to honor her mother's memory by choosing a path of healing and empowerment. Forgiveness allowed Jennifer to reclaim her narrative, finding closure on her own terms and setting herself on a course towards a brighter future.

As Jennifer looked ahead, she carried with her the lessons learned – the power of forgiveness, the value of healing, and the unwavering belief in the boundless possibilities that could be unlocked through the pursuit of emotional well-being. Her journey of healing was a testament to her strength, her resilience, and her unyielding determination to find closure, peace, and the capacity to embrace a future filled with hope and positivity.

Chapter 44: Media Spotlight

Jennifer's journey of entrepreneurship had been a testament to resilience, innovation, and unwavering determination. As "FinAI: Your Financial Companion" continued to make waves in the fintech landscape, Jennifer found herself thrust into the spotlight of media attention, her success story capturing the imaginations of journalists, influencers, and the public at large.

The journey from tragedy to triumph, from a young girl witnessing a devastating event to a successful entrepreneur empowering individuals through financial guidance, was a narrative that resonated deeply with people from all walks of life. Jennifer's ability to channel her pain into a mission of positive change had become an inspiration, capturing the attention of media outlets eager to share her remarkable story.

The media spotlight illuminated Jennifer's platform, "FinAI," as well as her personal journey of growth and empowerment. Journalists sought to understand the motivation behind "FinAI," the challenges Jennifer had overcome, and the impact her platform was making in the lives of users around the world.

Interviews, features, and documentaries began to circulate, each highlighting Jennifer's resilience, innovative approach, and dedication to creating meaningful change. Jennifer's ability to articulate her vision and share her experiences drew people in, inviting them to connect with her story on a personal level.

As media attention intensified, Jennifer found herself becoming a symbol of hope and possibility. Her story resonated with individuals who had faced their own hardships, inspiring them to persevere, pursue their passions, and embrace the power of positive change. The media spotlight transformed Jennifer into a role model, a beacon of possibility in a world that often seemed rife with challenges.

In the midst of the media frenzy, Jennifer remained grounded in her values and mission. She used the spotlight as an opportunity to raise awareness about responsible financial practices, the importance of financial literacy, and the need for ethical entrepreneurship. Jennifer's ability to leverage the attention for positive impact showcased her commitment to using her platform to make a difference.

While the media spotlight celebrated Jennifer's successes, it also highlighted the collective potential for positive change. Individuals around the world were inspired to take action, to pursue their dreams, and to create impact in their own communities. Jennifer's story became a catalyst for a ripple effect of empowerment, as people from diverse backgrounds were inspired to embrace their own journeys of growth and transformation.

As Jennifer looked ahead, she carried with her the lessons learned – the impact of media attention, the value of sharing one's story, and the unwavering belief in the boundless possibilities that could be unlocked through the pursuit of positive change. Her experience in the media spotlight was a testament to her resilience, her ability to inspire, and her unyielding determination to create a legacy that extended far beyond her own journey – a legacy of empowerment, hope, and the transformative power of resilience.

Chapter 45: Sharing Her Story

Jennifer's journey of transformation had not only propelled her into the world of entrepreneurship but had also ignited a powerful drive within her to inspire and uplift others. As the founder of "FinAI: Your Financial Companion," Jennifer recognized the opportunity to use her platform to advocate for resilience and empower individuals to overcome adversity.

Drawing upon her own experiences of triumph over tragedy, Jennifer became a passionate advocate for resilience. She understood that resilience was not just about bouncing back from challenges, but about harnessing inner strength, adapting to change, and using adversity as a catalyst for growth. Jennifer's journey was a testament to the extraordinary power of resilience, and she was determined to share this message with the world.

Jennifer embarked on a mission to connect with individuals and communities, both online and offline, to share her story and the lessons she had learned along the way. She participated in interviews, panel discussions, and speaking engagements, using each platform as an opportunity to inspire and empower others to embrace their own journeys of resilience.

One of the cornerstones of Jennifer's advocacy was her commitment to providing practical tools and resources for building resilience. Through partnerships with organizations, workshops, and webinars, Jennifer shared strategies for cultivating inner strength, managing stress, and navigating life's challenges with grace and determination. Her ability to translate her experiences into actionable advice resonated deeply with audiences around the world.

In addition to her public engagements, Jennifer used "FinAI" as a medium to spread her message of resilience. The platform featured a dedicated section that shared her personal journey, insights, and practical tips for overcoming adversity. Users of "FinAI" found not only financial guidance but also a source of inspiration and motivation to face life's challenges head-on.

Jennifer's advocacy for resilience extended to diverse communities, including schools, non-profits, and support groups. Her commitment to giving back and uplifting others demonstrated her belief in the transformative power of sharing one's story and providing a guiding light for those navigating their own paths.

As Jennifer looked ahead, she carried with her the lessons learned – the importance of advocating for resilience, the value of sharing one's story, and the unwavering belief in the boundless possibilities that could be unlocked through the pursuit of empowering others. Her advocacy efforts were a testament to her compassion, her leadership, and her unyielding determination to create a world where resilience was not just a quality but a way of life – a way of turning challenges into stepping stones towards a brighter, more empowered future.

Chapter 46: Philanthropic Ventures

Jennifer's journey of empowerment had not only transformed her life but had also ignited a deep sense of responsibility to give back to the community that had supported her along the way. As "FinAI: Your Financial Companion" continued to thrive, Jennifer recognized the profound opportunity to create lasting impact through philanthropy, channeling her success into initiatives that uplifted and empowered her community.

With a heart full of purpose, Jennifer established the "Empowerment Fund," a philanthropic initiative aimed at creating positive change in underserved communities. The fund's focus areas ranged from education and healthcare to entrepreneurship and social development, reflecting Jennifer's commitment to addressing a spectrum of needs.

One of the initiatives supported by the "Empowerment Fund" was the "Dreams Unlocked" scholarship program. Through this program, Jennifer provided scholarships to students from disadvantaged backgrounds, enabling them to pursue higher education and fulfill their aspirations. The program not only alleviated financial barriers but also served as a catalyst for change, empowering individuals to break the cycle of poverty and achieve their dreams.

In collaboration with local organizations, Jennifer launched the "Financial Freedom Workshops," a series of interactive sessions that equipped individuals with essential financial literacy skills. These workshops empowered participants to make informed financial decisions, build a strong foundation for their futures, and create a pathway towards financial independence.

The "Empowerment Fund" also supported budding entrepreneurs through the "Innovate for Impact" grant program. Jennifer recognized the transformative potential of entrepreneurship in driving economic growth and social change. By providing financial support and mentorship to innovative ventures with a focus on social impact, Jennifer empowered individuals to create businesses that not only generated profit but also made a meaningful difference in their communities.

In addition to financial contributions, Jennifer actively engaged in community service and volunteer efforts. She rallied her team at "FinAI" to participate in local initiatives, from environmental clean-ups to youth mentorship programs. Jennifer's commitment to hands-on involvement demonstrated her belief in the power of collective action and the profound impact that could be achieved through collaboration.

As the "Empowerment Fund" flourished, so did the ripple effects of Jennifer's philanthropic ventures. Communities were transformed, lives were uplifted, and a sense of hope and possibility pervaded. Jennifer's dedication to giving back was not just a reflection of her success; it was a reflection of her values, her compassion, and her unyielding determination to create a world where every individual had the opportunity to thrive.

Looking ahead, Jennifer carried with her the lessons learned – the importance of philanthropy, the value of giving back, and the unwavering belief in the boundless possibilities that could be unlocked through the pursuit of positive change. Her philanthropic ventures were a testament to her leadership, her empathy, and her unshakeable commitment to creating a legacy that extended far beyond business success – a legacy of empowerment, compassion, and the transformative power of philanthropy.

Chapter 47: Exploring New Avenues

Jennifer's journey of entrepreneurship had been marked by innovation, resilience, and an unwavering commitment to creating positive change. As "FinAI: Your Financial Companion" continued to thrive, Jennifer found herself at a crossroads, eager to explore new avenues and diversify her business interests, driven by a hunger for continued growth and impact.

Recognizing the dynamic landscape of opportunities, Jennifer embarked on a journey of exploration, seeking ways to expand her entrepreneurial horizons while staying true to her core values. Her success with "FinAI" had provided a strong foundation, and now Jennifer was ready to venture into new territories.

One of the avenues Jennifer explored was the world of sustainable technology. With a growing emphasis on environmental consciousness, Jennifer saw an opportunity to leverage her expertise in finance and technology to create innovative solutions that addressed pressing environmental challenges. She founded "GreenTech Innovations," a company dedicated to developing sustainable technologies that had the potential to revolutionize industries and mitigate the impact of climate change.

Through "GreenTech Innovations," Jennifer spearheaded projects that ranged from renewable energy solutions to waste reduction initiatives. Her commitment to sustainability was not only a strategic business move but also a reflection of her values and her determination to create a positive impact on the planet.

In addition to sustainable technology, Jennifer diversified her interests by entering the world of social entrepreneurship. She co-founded "EmpowerHER," a social enterprise focused on empowering women through education, mentorship, and economic opportunities. The initiative aimed to bridge gender disparities and create pathways for women to thrive in various industries.

Jennifer's foray into new avenues was not without challenges. Each venture required meticulous planning, strategic partnerships, and a willingness to adapt and learn. Yet, Jennifer's ability to navigate uncharted waters demonstrated her agility as an entrepreneur and her unwavering commitment to pushing the boundaries of what was possible.

As her business interests diversified, Jennifer's impact also expanded. The success of "GreenTech Innovations" contributed to a cleaner and more sustainable future, while "EmpowerHER" was instrumental in creating opportunities for women to excel and lead in traditionally male-dominated fields.

Jennifer's ability to explore new avenues while staying true to her values showcased her entrepreneurial prowess and her determination to leave a lasting legacy of positive change. Her journey of diversification was a testament to her resilience, her innovation, and her unyielding belief in the boundless possibilities that could be unlocked through the pursuit of new horizons.

Looking ahead, Jennifer carried with her the lessons learned – the importance of diversification, the value of exploring new avenues, and the unwavering belief in the boundless possibilities that could be unlocked through the pursuit of continuous growth and impact. Her ventures into new territories were a testament to her entrepreneurial spirit, her commitment to innovation, and her unshakeable determination to create a legacy that extended far beyond her initial successes – a legacy of transformative entrepreneurship and a relentless pursuit of positive change.

Chapter 48: Overcoming Burnout

Jennifer's journey of entrepreneurship had been defined by ambition, resilience, and an unwavering commitment to creating positive change. As her ventures continued to flourish, Jennifer found herself grappling with a new challenge – the demanding nature of her multifaceted responsibilities, which threatened to lead her down the path of burnout.

Balancing the demands of "FinAI: Your Financial Companion," "GreenTech Innovations," and "EmpowerHER," along with her philanthropic efforts and advocacy work, had become a monumental task. Jennifer's passion and dedication were boundless, but she realized that sustaining her pace without proper self-care could lead to exhaustion and burnout.

Recognizing the importance of addressing this issue head-on, Jennifer embarked on a journey to reclaim balance in her life. She sought guidance from mentors, consulted with experts, and engaged in introspection to identify strategies for managing her responsibilities while safeguarding her well-being.

Jennifer's journey towards overcoming burnout began with setting clear boundaries. She established designated work hours, allowing herself time for rest, rejuvenation, and quality moments with loved ones. By delineating work and personal time, Jennifer created a framework that prevented her from becoming overwhelmed by the demands of her various ventures.

Incorporating self-care practices became a cornerstone of Jennifer's routine. She prioritized activities that nurtured her physical, mental, and emotional well-being, from exercise and meditation to spending time in nature and indulging in hobbies she loved. These practices not only recharged her energy but also provided moments of reflection and inner peace.

Delegation emerged as a vital tool in Jennifer's quest for balance. Recognizing that she couldn't do it all alone, Jennifer empowered her teams at "FinAI," "GreenTech Innovations," and "EmpowerHER" to take on increased responsibilities. Delegating tasks not only alleviated Jennifer's workload but also fostered a sense of empowerment among her team members.

Jennifer's journey to overcome burnout was also marked by a shift in perspective. She learned to celebrate small victories, acknowledge her limitations, and embrace imperfection. By letting go of the pressure to be constantly perfect, Jennifer allowed herself the freedom to focus on what truly mattered – making a meaningful impact while preserving her own well-being.

The process of overcoming burnout was not without its challenges. It required discipline, self-awareness, and a commitment to ongoing self-care. However, Jennifer's determination to strike a balance between her demanding responsibilities and her personal well-being demonstrated her resilience, her adaptability, and her unyielding belief in the importance of sustaining herself for the long journey ahead.

As Jennifer looked ahead, she carried with her the lessons learned – the significance of balance, the value of self-care, and the unwavering belief in the boundless possibilities that could be unlocked through the pursuit of a harmonious and sustainable life. Her journey of overcoming burnout was a testament to her leadership, her resilience, and her unshakeable determination to create a legacy that encompassed not only her entrepreneurial ventures but also her own well-being and fulfillment.

Chapter 49: Unexpected Alliances

Jennifer's entrepreneurial journey had been characterized by innovation, resilience, and an unwavering commitment to creating positive change. As "FinAI: Your Financial Companion," "GreenTech Innovations," and "EmpowerHER" continued to thrive, Jennifer found herself embarking on a series of unexpected alliances – collaborations with partners that were as surprising as they were transformative.

The notion of unexpected alliances had always intrigued Jennifer. She believed that by bringing together diverse perspectives, industries, and expertise, new avenues of innovation and impact could be unlocked. With this philosophy in mind, Jennifer set out to forge partnerships that transcended traditional boundaries.

One of Jennifer's most unexpected collaborations came in the form of a collaboration between "FinAI" and a renowned art foundation. Together, they launched the "Art x Finance" initiative, a project that aimed to bridge the worlds of art and finance, creating a platform where artists could gain financial literacy and access financial resources while infusing the finance sector with creativity and artistic inspiration.

The collaboration saw the creation of a series of workshops, exhibitions, and mentorship programs that brought together artists, financial experts, and entrepreneurs. The initiative not only empowered artists to navigate the financial landscape but also inspired financial professionals to think creatively and embrace artistic expression in their work.

In another surprising partnership, Jennifer joined forces with a well-established pharmaceutical company to launch "HealthTech Innovations." This collaboration aimed to leverage technology and healthcare expertise to develop innovative solutions that improved patient outcomes and accessibility to healthcare services. The fusion of finance, technology, and healthcare resulted in groundbreaking advancements that had a profound impact on the lives of individuals in underserved communities.

Jennifer's ability to collaborate with partners from diverse industries was a testament to her open-mindedness, her visionary thinking, and her commitment to creating holistic and multifaceted solutions to complex challenges. These unexpected alliances not only expanded her business horizons but also reinforced her belief in the transformative power of collaboration.

As Jennifer looked ahead, she carried with her the lessons learned – the importance of unexpected alliances, the value of collaboration, and the unwavering belief in the boundless possibilities that could be unlocked through the pursuit of innovative partnerships. Her ventures into unexpected alliances were a testament to her visionary thinking, her adaptability, and her unshakeable determination to create a legacy that extended far beyond her own ventures – a legacy of interdisciplinary collaboration, transformative innovation, and a relentless pursuit of positive change.

Chapter 50: Business Innovations

Jennifer's entrepreneurial journey had been marked by a relentless pursuit of innovation, a commitment to positive change, and a determination to create impact across industries. As "FinAI: Your Financial Companion," "GreenTech Innovations," and "EmpowerHER" continued to thrive, Jennifer found herself on the cutting edge of business innovations, disrupting her industries and paving the way for transformative change.

With each venture, Jennifer pushed the boundaries of what was possible. In the realm of fintech, "FinAI" continued to evolve, introducing revolutionary features that enhanced user experiences, provided personalized financial guidance, and utilized cutting-edge artificial intelligence to empower individuals to make informed decisions about their finances.

"GreenTech Innovations" remained at the forefront of sustainable technology, introducing groundbreaking solutions that addressed pressing environmental challenges. From innovative renewable energy sources to eco-friendly manufacturing processes, Jennifer's team pushed the boundaries of technological advancements while championing a greener and more sustainable future.

"EmpowerHER" had grown into a global force for gender equality, introducing initiatives that empowered women in every corner of the world. Mentorship programs, leadership summits, and economic empowerment initiatives were just a few of the ways in which "EmpowerHER" disrupted traditional gender norms and transformed the landscape of female leadership.

Jennifer's ability to disrupt her industries was not limited to her existing ventures. She continually sought out new opportunities for innovation and positive impact. Jennifer's dedication to pushing the envelope led to the creation of "Tech for Good Labs," an incubator that supported startups and entrepreneurs focused on using technology for social and environmental change.

Through "Tech for Good Labs," Jennifer fostered a community of like-minded innovators who shared a vision for leveraging technology to create a better world. The incubator provided resources, mentorship, and funding to startups that were developing solutions to address challenges ranging from healthcare accessibility to education inequality.

Jennifer's commitment to disrupting her industries was driven by a vision of a future where positive change was not just a possibility, but a reality. Her ability to envision and execute innovative strategies showcased her leadership, her tenacity, and her unwavering belief in the boundless possibilities that could be unlocked through the pursuit of disruptive business practices.

As Jennifer looked ahead, she carried with her the lessons learned – the importance of business innovation, the value of disruption, and the unwavering belief in the boundless possibilities that could be unlocked through the pursuit of transformative change. Her ventures into business innovations were a testament to her visionary thinking, her adaptability, and her unshakeable determination to create a legacy that extended far beyond her own ventures – a legacy of groundbreaking entrepreneurship, transformative impact, and a relentless pursuit of positive change.

Chapter 51: New Challenges

Jennifer's journey of entrepreneurship had been characterized by resilience, innovation, and an unwavering commitment to positive change. As "FinAI: Your Financial Companion," "GreenTech Innovations," and "EmpowerHER" continued to thrive, Jennifer encountered a new set of challenges – economic downturns that tested her resolve and pushed her to navigate uncharted waters.

The global economy experienced a period of uncertainty, marked by financial volatility, market fluctuations, and economic instability. Jennifer's ventures were not immune to the effects of these challenges. As businesses struggled to adapt and consumers faced financial constraints, Jennifer found herself facing a landscape that demanded creativity, adaptability, and strategic thinking.

The economic downturns presented Jennifer with a unique opportunity to draw upon her entrepreneurial spirit and problem-solving skills. She recognized that navigating these challenges required a multi-faceted approach that encompassed both short-term solutions and long-term strategies.

One of Jennifer's immediate actions was to strengthen the financial resilience of her ventures. She engaged in a comprehensive review of her business operations, identifying areas for cost optimization, resource allocation, and operational efficiency. By streamlining processes and focusing on core strengths, Jennifer ensured that her ventures remained agile and well-equipped to weather the storm.

Jennifer also leveraged her network of mentors, advisors, and industry experts to gain insights into navigating economic downturns. Collaborating with thought leaders, she devised strategies that positioned her ventures for resilience and growth, even in the face of adversity.

In response to shifting consumer behaviors and market dynamics, Jennifer introduced creative solutions to adapt her ventures. "FinAI" rolled out tailored financial guidance to help users manage their finances during uncertain times. "GreenTech Innovations" pivoted towards sustainable products and services that aligned with evolving consumer preferences. "EmpowerHER" launched virtual programs and initiatives that empowered women to thrive in new remote work environments.

Throughout the challenges posed by economic downturns, Jennifer's ability to lead with resilience, adaptability, and strategic foresight shone brightly. Her commitment to problem-solving and her capacity to embrace change were a testament to her entrepreneurial prowess and her unwavering belief in the boundless possibilities that could be unlocked through the pursuit of innovative solutions.

As Jennifer looked ahead, she carried with her the lessons learned – the importance of adaptability, the value of strategic thinking, and the unwavering belief in the boundless possibilities that could be unlocked through the pursuit of resilience in the face of adversity. Her navigation of economic downturns was a testament to her leadership, her agility, and her unshakeable determination to create a legacy that encompassed not only her entrepreneurial ventures but also her ability to navigate and overcome challenges with grace and innovation.

Chapter 52: Adapting and Thriving

Jennifer's entrepreneurial journey had been marked by innovation, resilience, and an unwavering commitment to positive change. As "FinAI: Your Financial Companion," "GreenTech Innovations," and "EmpowerHER" faced the challenges of economic downturns, Jennifer demonstrated her ability to adapt and lead her ventures through storms, emerging stronger and more determined than ever before.

The storms that battered the global economy were met with Jennifer's unwavering resolve. Recognizing that challenges were an inherent part of the entrepreneurial landscape, she harnessed her strategic acumen and embraced a mindset of adaptability.

Jennifer's ventures were not simply bystanders in the face of adversity; they were beacons of innovation that illuminated the path forward. She led her teams with a spirit of unity, rallying them around a shared purpose of navigating challenges and finding opportunities within them.

In response to the economic downturns, Jennifer's leadership was characterized by three key pillars: resilience, innovation, and empathy.

Resilience: Jennifer's ventures demonstrated remarkable resilience by recalibrating their strategies and operations. She led her teams in fortifying their foundations, ensuring that each venture was well-positioned to weather the storms. This resilience was evident in the measured approach to financial management, cost optimization, and strategic decision-making.

Innovation: Economic downturns spurred Jennifer's ventures to innovate at an accelerated pace. "FinAI" introduced new features that provided users with real-time financial insights to navigate uncertain times. "GreenTech Innovations" leveraged its expertise to create eco-friendly products that resonated with environmentally conscious consumers. "EmpowerHER" pioneered virtual platforms that brought empowerment programs to women around the world, transcending geographical limitations.

Empathy: Jennifer's commitment to empathy and understanding was a cornerstone of her leadership. She recognized that her ventures were not just businesses, but vehicles for positive impact. By aligning her ventures with the evolving needs of users, customers, and communities, Jennifer ensured that her endeavors remained deeply connected to the people they served.

Through her leadership, Jennifer's ventures not only weathered the storms of economic downturns but emerged from them as stronger and more resilient entities. The challenges became catalysts for growth, propelling her ventures to new heights of innovation and impact.

As Jennifer looked ahead, she carried with her the lessons learned – the importance of resilience, the value of innovation, and the unwavering belief in the boundless possibilities that could be unlocked through the pursuit of adaptability in the face of adversity. Her ability to lead her ventures through storms was a testament to her visionary thinking, her unwavering determination, and her unshakeable commitment to creating a legacy that extended far beyond her own successes – a legacy of resilience, innovation, and the transformative power of leadership in challenging times.

Chapter 53: A Personal Triumph

Jennifer's journey of entrepreneurship had been defined by resilience, innovation, and an unwavering commitment to positive change. As "FinAI: Your Financial Companion," "GreenTech Innovations," and "EmpowerHER" continued to thrive, Jennifer reached a significant milestone that marked not only a business achievement but a deeply personal triumph.

The milestone that Jennifer achieved was not just about numbers or recognition; it was a testament to her unwavering dedication, her unrelenting pursuit of excellence, and her ability to overcome challenges. It was a milestone that showcased her growth as an entrepreneur and her profound impact on the world around her.

After years of tireless effort and unwavering determination, "FinAI: Your Financial Companion" reached one million users worldwide. This achievement was not just a reflection of the platform's popularity, but a testament to the lives it had transformed, the financial guidance it had provided, and the empowerment it had facilitated.

For Jennifer, the milestone was a personal triumph that carried with it a deep sense of fulfillment. It was a validation of her vision, a realization of her dreams, and a realization of the positive change she had set out to create in the world.

As Jennifer celebrated this achievement, she reflected on the journey that had led her here. She thought about the challenges she had overcome, the lessons she had learned, and the unwavering support of her team, mentors, and collaborators. Each step of the way, Jennifer had remained true to her values, her vision, and her commitment to making a difference.

The milestone was not just an endpoint, but a new beginning – a springboard for even greater achievements and impact. Jennifer's personal triumph inspired her to continue pushing the boundaries, exploring new horizons, and creating positive change in the lives of individuals and communities around the world.

Looking ahead, Jennifer carried with her the lessons learned – the importance of perseverance, the value of vision, and the unwavering belief in the boundless possibilities that could be unlocked through the pursuit of personal triumphs. Her achievement of reaching one million users was a testament to her leadership, her resilience, and her unshakeable determination to create a legacy that encompassed not only her entrepreneurial ventures but also her personal growth, her transformation, and her ability to inspire others to achieve their own triumphs in the pursuit of positive change.

Chapter 54: Reconnecting with Love

Jennifer's entrepreneurial journey had been a testament to her resilience, innovation, and unwavering commitment to creating positive change. Amidst the demands of "FinAI: Your Financial Companion," "GreenTech Innovations," and "EmpowerHER," Jennifer found herself experiencing a significant evolution in her romantic relationship – a journey of reconnection and growth that mirrored her own transformation.

As her ventures continued to thrive, Jennifer reconnected with an old friend from her university days, Alex. Their paths had crossed unexpectedly at a social event, reigniting a connection that had once been strong. Alex, an entrepreneur himself, shared Jennifer's passion for creating positive change in the world and admired her dedication to her ventures.

Jennifer and Alex's rekindled connection blossomed into a deep and meaningful romantic relationship. Their shared values, mutual support, and understanding of the demands of entrepreneurship created a strong foundation for their evolving partnership.

Navigating the complexities of their romantic relationship alongside their entrepreneurial pursuits was a journey that required open communication, empathy, and a willingness to embrace vulnerability. Jennifer and Alex's ability to balance their personal lives with their professional aspirations showcased their maturity and their commitment to nurturing a relationship that added depth and fulfillment to their lives.

Through their journey of reconnection, Jennifer and Alex became each other's pillars of support, celebrating each other's successes, and providing solace during moments of challenge. They found solace in the midst of their busy lives, sharing moments of laughter, quiet reflection, and unwavering encouragement.

Their relationship also served as a reminder of the importance of self-care and the need to maintain a harmonious work-life balance. Jennifer and Alex's shared experiences inspired them to prioritize their well-being, nurturing not only their ventures but also their personal growth and happiness.

As Jennifer and Alex's romantic relationship evolved, it became a testament to the power of love, connection, and understanding. Their journey of reconnection mirrored Jennifer's own transformation – a journey marked by resilience, growth, and a commitment to positive change.

Looking ahead, Jennifer carried with her the lessons learned – the importance of connection, the value of nurturing relationships, and the unwavering belief in the boundless possibilities that could be unlocked through the pursuit of love and partnership. Her evolving romantic relationship was a testament to her emotional intelligence, her ability to navigate complexities, and her unshakeable determination to create a legacy that encompassed not only her entrepreneurial ventures but also the depth of her personal connections and the transformative power of love.

Chapter 55: Looking Ahead

Jennifer stood at a pivotal juncture in her entrepreneurial journey, a vantage point that allowed her to reflect on the path she had traversed and contemplate the vast landscape of future endeavors that lay before her. As "FinAI: Your Financial Companion," "GreenTech Innovations," and "EmpowerHER" continued to thrive, Jennifer's mind was alive with possibilities, dreams, and aspirations for what lay ahead.

The achievements and challenges of her past ventures had equipped Jennifer with a profound sense of purpose and a thirst for continuous growth. She found herself contemplating the legacy she wanted to leave behind – a legacy that extended beyond her individual successes and encompassed a broader vision of positive change.

Jennifer envisioned a future where her impact resonated on a global scale, where her endeavors reached new heights of innovation, and where her commitment to social and environmental progress blazed a trail for others to follow. Her journey of empowerment had taught her that the pursuit of positive change was a lifelong endeavor, one that required constant adaptation, innovation, and an unyielding belief in the transformative power of entrepreneurship.

With the wisdom gained from her experiences, Jennifer identified new areas of exploration that fueled her passion for positive change. She contemplated the creation of an "EmpowerMENT" foundation, a platform that would amplify the voices of marginalized communities and provide resources for empowerment, education, and entrepreneurship.

Jennifer's vision also extended to fostering collaboration between governments, corporations, and civil society organizations to drive sustainable development and social impact on a global scale. She imagined herself at the forefront of initiatives that tackled some of the world's most pressing challenges – from poverty eradication and gender equality to environmental conservation and technological innovation.

Amidst her contemplation of future endeavors, Jennifer remained grounded in her commitment to personal growth, resilience, and well-being. She recognized that her ability to drive change was intrinsically linked to her own journey of transformation – a journey that required nurturing her own physical, mental, and emotional well-being.

As Jennifer looked ahead, she carried with her the lessons learned – the importance of vision, the value of innovation, and the unwavering belief in the boundless possibilities that could be unlocked through the pursuit of positive change. Her contemplation of future endeavors was a testament to her visionary thinking, her adaptability, and her unshakeable determination to create a legacy that extended far beyond her own successes – a legacy of transformative entrepreneurship, global impact, and a relentless pursuit of creating a better world for generations to come.

Chapter 56: Inspiring the Next Generation

Jennifer's journey of entrepreneurship had been characterized by resilience, innovation, and an unwavering commitment to positive change. As "FinAI: Your Financial Companion," "GreenTech Innovations," and "EmpowerHER" continued to thrive, Jennifer found herself embracing a new role – that of a mentor to young and aspiring entrepreneurs who sought to follow in her footsteps.

Recognizing the power of mentorship and the impact it could have on shaping the future of entrepreneurship, Jennifer launched the "RiseUp Mentorship Program." This initiative aimed to provide guidance, support, and inspiration to young individuals who were eager to embark on their own entrepreneurial journeys.

Through the "RiseUp Mentorship Program," Jennifer opened her doors to a diverse group of mentees, each with their unique aspirations, challenges, and dreams. Jennifer's approach to mentorship was characterized by empathy, authenticity, and a genuine desire to empower the next generation of changemakers.

One of Jennifer's mentees, Maya, was a young woman with a passion for environmental conservation. With Jennifer's guidance, Maya launched her own eco-friendly product line and initiated community engagement projects that aimed to raise awareness about the importance of sustainability.

Another mentee, Raj, had a vision of leveraging technology to provide educational opportunities to underserved communities. Jennifer's mentorship helped Raj secure partnerships and funding for his innovative e-learning platform, which transformed the lives of countless students who lacked access to quality education.

As Jennifer shared her experiences, insights, and lessons learned, she witnessed the transformative impact of mentorship on her mentees.

The "RiseUp Mentorship Program" became a breeding ground for innovation, resilience, and a shared commitment to positive change.

Jennifer's dedication to inspiring the next generation extended beyond one-on-one mentorship sessions. She organized workshops, webinars, and networking events that provided young entrepreneurs with access to resources, knowledge, and a supportive community of like-minded individuals.

Through her mentorship efforts, Jennifer found herself not only empowering others but also fueling her own sense of purpose. Seeing her mentees flourish, innovate, and create positive change ignited a new wave of motivation within her – a reminder of the profound impact that mentorship could have on shaping the future of entrepreneurship and societal progress.

As Jennifer looked ahead, she carried with her the lessons learned – the importance of mentorship, the value of paying it forward, and the unwavering belief in the boundless possibilities that could be unlocked through the pursuit of inspiring the next generation. Her commitment to mentoring young entrepreneurs was a testament to her leadership, her empathy, and her unshakeable determination to create a legacy that encompassed not only her entrepreneurial ventures but also her ability to uplift, guide, and empower the leaders of tomorrow.

Milton Keynes UK
Ingram Content Group UK Ltd.
UKHW011948160224
437951UK00001B/80

9 798224 415434